JONAGOLD

PETER BLENDELL

Copyright © 2014 by Peter Blendell
First Edition – February 2014

ISBN
978-1-4602-3163-0 (Hardcover)
978-1-4602-3164-7 (Paperback)
978-1-4602-3165-4 (eBook)

All rights reserved.

No part of this publication may be reproduced in any form, or by any means, electronic or mechanical, including photocopying, recording, or any information browsing, storage, or retrieval system, without permission in writing from the publisher.

Produced by:

FriesenPress
Suite 300 – 852 Fort Street
Victoria, BC, Canada V8W 1H8

www.friesenpress.com

Distributed to the trade by The Ingram Book Company

Table of Contents

Adam	1
David	33
Gail	69

Adam

October third was a clear, cool morning. Up early, start early? 'Let's do it.'
Three creaks of the hinges, three slaps of the door, and we were outside. Six feet, crossing the porch and stepping down, took us onto the driveway: a raggedy little bunch, gearing ourselves up to go. Momentarily, ...any minute now, ...we will ...
Instead we stood, as we do some days: yawny and slow, on the gravel and clumped-up leaves. First shuffling, then still, we took in the near-frost morning.
Quiet, mist low on the cut-but-not-baled west field: rolling, hanging, quiet... then geese: a flapping, grating thousand - they roughed up the silver-skinned millpond with their lift-off.
I listened, and rolled my neck. David bent down to fix a sock. He straightened himself back up, and that was it. Waiting time was done.
'Gentlemen...' Gail got us moving, as she will. '...shall we...?'
A nod from me, and we did. Turned to face north, and off to work.

I swung my arms, front to back, as we walked, three in a row. Sun behind the poplars; our long shadows running ahead. I clapped lightly, palms just touching; and turned my head: back at the sunlight and dark branch pattern, and ahead to our shadow shapes on the dirt tracks and crunchy grass. At the top of the laneway, we each took a bushel-basket from the stack, and moved left-to-right to look along the rows for the planks we'd leaned up to mark the last tree we'd worked the day before. There's mine...
It soon warmed up into another fine day for picking, and by noon we were done. Eight boxes: our best crop so far, and near to as good a one as we could have hoped for. The big boxes sat pigglty-scattered in the flat field below the trees—wherever we'd set them to begin with. That was fine with

me, for now, but Gail wanted our work on display and looking just-right. She brought the loader up to right-in-front-of each box, and needled the forks in under. Delicate work, and done with no haste. It was fair entertainment, and I gave it the patience it wanted. Eventually, she got them all wrestled into line: side by each, and spaced about the same distance apart. Only a few piled-up-too-high-anyway apples rolled off in the process.

David watched her careful driving for a minute, looked back at the orchard, and then up at a southbound chevron wheeling in low for a landing on the pond. He seemed to give all three equal consideration. He got a feedbag from the flatbed and went back down the rows gathering up fruit we'd missed or rejected. I took off my hat, thought what a nice morning it was, and ran a hand through my hair.

Gail parked the loader back where it came from, and walked over slowly, like somebody enjoying the luxury of taking her time. She unsnapped her vest and tilted her hat back on her head. It was a good imitation of the 'farmer-takes-a-break' routine, and she glanced over to be sure I appreciated her talent. David came back with a half sack-full and one in his teeth, stooping every so often to pick up one of Gail's spills. When he came up to where we were, we all three stood there in a ragged row admiring the neat row. The apples sat pink and gold and shiny above the angled-out rims of the new plywood boxes. We kept admiring, and the sky poured blue in my eyes till it was all they could hold... full blue, and David at ten was ashamed that he couldn't help tearing up when Smoky came back with a mouse and growled and chewed on its head... and today again, where the maples running up the far side of Burrit's lane were a solid bank of glory: red, gold and green.

It was good farming, and almost done for the year; we felt proud and pleased. I called 'lunch', and turned to go back. David chose a couple he liked from the feedbag, got his shovel from the flatbed, and loped over to dig them in by the pink rock where Sam was buried. I picked up the feedbag.

Gail and I walked back down to the laneway, silent and just walking, and she wondered a question, in her way, without looking at me. 'You never said how you got into apples.' I heard the words and started thinking while she finished. 'Everybody else is getting out.'

Her city voice filled my ears, ...a breeze, a rustle, a buzz..., and I heard dad imitating the sound of an automatic choke cutting out when he taught me to drive.

'Keep your foot off the throttle till you hear it rev down like that...'

Things happen to me. I don't understand them or cause them. It can take a minute to figure out what's really going on. Why we planted or why I didn't say? I turned back to ask, but she'd turned back too, and was calling David.

'Come on; lunch.'

I unturned, waved to mom on the porch, and kept walking.

Gail left her gumboots in the mudroom, and went on through the breezeway to check our messages. I went inside, poked my head in the kitchen and held out the feedbag.

'We're here, with apples.' Mom was taking hotdogs out of the water. Her hair was bright blue and puffed out, and she looked at me looking surprised.

'Don't say anything.'

I shrugged. 'OK, I won't, but I'd like to.'

No need to, either: Steph had obviously used her as a guinea pig for Hair Today's latest trainee. Mom was setting the table, ready to press ahead in spite of any delay. 'Where is everybody? David's hotdogs are ready. I'm starved.'

She started serving out soup into the blue bowls, and Gail came back in from our apartment. 'John called back. He can press tomorrow if we get there first thing. Sharp, Alma. None of that wimpy light blue rinse blue, eh?'

She looked over at the bag on the floor. 'Sauce, pie, or jelly?'

Mom put out the dish of applesauce, answered 'Make a request…', and I sat down. David came in and got his relish from the fridge and sat down in his place with the two hotdogs lined up just so on the white plate. He squeezed relish on one side of the pair, and spooned applesauce from the dish on the other. His place looked out: west, over the porch and on to what the season showed. He checked his work for neat before he cut it up. I salted my soup and made conversation.

'What do you think of Mom's hair, David?'

He'd been watching the sky and chewing and maybe hoping to see the geese make another pass at the pond; he turned to look.

'Mom likes blue.'

He smiled a little, pleased with himself, as he worked out the rest of his line. 'I do too.'

Gail caught the smile and looked over at me. 'How about you?'

David's little smile widened slowly to big, and I looked around from smile to smile and the smell of soup and apples filled the kitchen, …and mom when she still had her force and straight blue-black hair and mine then carrot, …and David at seven couldn't sit still. He ran through the house, bounced off chairs, and banged the piano. Mom set her mouth. She looked at dad to see if he'd speak first. David ran back in, waved his arms, and sang.

'...I'm a goose, goose I am ...'

Dad frowned, stared down, and went back to eating. Mom stood.

'David.'

She took his raised arm as he ran by. Her hand held his small one gently, but firmly. She let go when he stopped, and he stood with arms raised, fingers fluttering, looking up at her. She didn't yet understand that no amount of force would change things. Gently, but firmly, she explained the matter. 'We said no running in the house. You agreed. Do you remember?' He lowered his arms.

'I'm not running; I'm flying...'

That did it. Dad stood up too, solid and tall and growling, and glared down at him. 'No running, no waving, and no silly singing. It's all forbidden. We don't want to hear it. Ever.'

More frightened tears; another silent lunch. The old kitchen then with both pump and taps on the brown counter. Lino. Pump to the side of the sink, taps behind, and now the white new room, where mom was talking about her visit to the hairdresser. '...young to be trusted alone with the scissors, but Stephanie...'

It was almost eleven when Gail went to sleep. I got up and opened the window; night flowed in. I stood, smelled sharp-edged frost, and looked at me in the upper panes. A face, a fall air breath; drawn-in full. I saw piled-high pink and gold apples, blue sky and blue hair, and remembered Gail's question. I don't know how things happen when they're happening. With other people, it's all fast. For me, they unfold in parts, one at a time. I watch and try to deal with them that way—step by step. Do other folks shape the way things turn out? React, right when they happen? Deep sky, wheeling stars, and growing apples...Where did it start? How to say? Pick a point in the past...or an event. Say, graduation day: see dad hurting in those months, mom efficient and worried, David now quiet and nervous, ...that's how it happens, for me. The sound of 'You never said how you got into apples?' and wind in my ears and blue in my eyes. One scene jostles the next into place, with it all eventually leading to an answer someplace, but by then everybody's long since left me behind, telling the story to myself.

To myself, now into apples. That now twenty year ago day. Locusts in flower. More chores for me. How David didn't really get it. Graduation. Shining my shoes...one leads to the next. This late there's nothing to stop the procession. Burrit's maples are the darkest shape in the night window. I smell the moving cold air and the maples stand there: lined-up, even-spaced, ...old. Me. Them. Watching each other. This frost will kill the clover...

I went back to bed, the wind kept filling my ears, and I graduated from PECI June 29, 1989, and hoped it would be the last time I saw the place. We never clicked. Totally boring, but if I kept my head down nobody bothered me, which is how it played out. Auto shop was ok, but it was stuff I mostly knew already, so it amounted to more of the same. They did try to teach us some diagnostics on the computer, but it always crashed. It was old Mr A's last year teaching, and he felt the same way I did about the place. He said back when he'd learned the trade they took a car apart and put it back together, and what a good way that was, ...and ducked outside for a smoke.

Cory Miller remembered a not-that-badly-beat-up '76 Regal in his dad's wrecking yard, and we jumped it late Sunday night and drove it into town. No plates, no insurance. We climbed the west fence, got in and worked our way out to the road with just a flashlight. Somebody had bought the windshield, and the back window was shot out at some point. That had left a six inch or so hole with spider lines and shards hanging loose, so it was a noisy, breezy ride. The foam in the upholstery had gone moldy, and a little crop sprouted up in the back seat. The burdock was doing nicely. We were damp-pantsed and dirty by the time we got the Regal parked outside the bay door of the auto shop, and when we forced the rusty doors shut they made an awful rasping sound in the empty lot. Then we looked at each other and cracked up—we were so carried away with the fun of stealing a car that we hadn't thought about getting back home.

Cory kicked the door, but he was wearing sneakers, and just pretending to lose his temper with himself. 'Pretty sharp auto rustlers, eh?'

Town was silent and deserted as we walked back to Main St. The maples were leafed out, the lights in most of the houses were off, and we could hardly see where we were headed on the back streets. We walked side by side down Bridge St, and when we turned onto Union a car came by and Cory waved, but it didn't stop, and took the left fork on out to Glenora.

Heading up the hill I looked back, and saw another set of lights coming down Union. 'Car', and we turned around to try again. It took the right fork towards us, we stuck our thumbs out, and as it turned uphill an OPP cruiser took shape. Cory looked at me- 'shit'—and then at the big white Crown Vic as it slowed up. 'Don't say anything. They can't prove it was us.'

It was too late for me to answer—it pulled over ahead of us, and gave a quick, friendly pop of its cherry. Cory opened the front passenger door, and we both looked in, and saw Constable Taylor, with all her cop gear piled on the front seat. Even tied back in a ponytail, her red hair looked too big for the rest of her, and made it feel less like a cop talking. 'What are you fellows doing out so late?'

We were both standing next to the open door, but Cory was sort of in front of me. 'Helping Adam's aunt. Change a fan belt.'

I thought that answer had a lot of potential problems, but now we were stuck with it. She didn't check for flaws. 'Hop in the back. I can ride you as far as the turnoff.'

She knew Cory's dad from the time a guy from Napanee tried to sell him a nearly new Jimmy for two grand, 'cash'. Mr M had Cory call it in to her while he pretended to do a thorough look-see on it.

'You two smell like more you've been swamp-wading than fixing fan belts.'

Cory was quick on the draw. 'That's just Adam. He's sort of ...not completely housebroken.' I elbowed him, and she laughed. 'How's your dad?'

Now that it looked like we weren't about to get busted, Cory relaxed. 'ok.' A pause. 'They went to a wedding in Sterling today.' I remembered her first name. Maureen. Dad said they moved the constables around so they didn't make too close friends with the locals.

The radio crackled, and she picked up the speaker. 'Thirty One...3-1'

I couldn't make out what they were saying, but she must have. 'Oh, I know it; know it all too well...ok. One quick little errand first and I'm on it...yeah, over.' She put the speaker back on the hook and chuckled. '...got to put the dog in or she's after the neighbours' chickens. Again.' I liked the sound of her laughing and thought that I hadn't heard much of it around our house lately.

She dropped us at the Black River cut-off, and turned down the hill. We both seemed inclined to do the same thing that night. We stood still and watched her taillights fade, turned and looked at each other and up at the moon for a second, and started walking. Puffy clouds raced along above us, and then everything went dark. The locusts along the road wouldn't leaf in for a month yet, and when the moon came out from behind the clouds again it lit everything up,—the clouds made a purple and grey quilted pattern gliding along behind the silhouette of the twisty branches. Our walking made a tiny sound in the huge night when we scuffed the gravel along the side of the road. Cory turned off in his driveway; and spoke as he headed toward the house.

'Tomorrow, buddy.'

'It's already tomorrow....'

'Well, later, then?'

'Take care.'

I kept going, and turned into our drive. The wind was in my face, with tomorrow's rain on it. The pole which should have braced the door to the driveshed had blown down, and when the moon came out, there was Sam standing in the doorway—it was bright enough to see his black nostrils moving as he smelled tomorrow's rain, too. Or today's.... I nudged him back all into the shed, closed the door and wedged the brace back in place. I was tired. 'Call it a night', I remembered, and went inside and to bed as quietly as I could.

The next week we all had fun with the taking-the-car-apart phase of the operation, and scattering parts all over the shop. The week after that Mr A was sick and the week after that was graduation. The end of the story of high school, and the parted-out Regal lay there spread out in a god-awful mess on the last day. Cory took the radio and his dad wanted the pads and rotors back. He looked at the junk on the floor and benches and a section of the dash on the drill press, where a hole-saw had got bound-up on it and the whole thing just been left there, bent onto the stem of the press. He shook his head.

'Help yourself, amigo. Never know when something might come in handy.' I took the antenna for the half-ton, and the starter motor because you always need one eventually, and—since it was unbolted and just sitting there—the power steering pump. There was nobody around to ask permission from, and it felt maybe-not-quite-right at first, but I couldn't really find any harm in it.

Mr Miller gave us a ride home, and he didn't seem to see any, either. 'That's all you boys could pick off that carcass? Lazy pair of buzzards you make.'

Graduation morning Mom was at it early, getting everybody spruced up and moving in the right direction. 'I'm so proud of you, Adam. Comb your hair down. Doesn't he look smart, Don?'

Dad took a T-3, and Mom got David dressed up in a tie and one of Dad's old jackets. She called her sister to tell her to make sure Amanda remembered to take a picture of me getting my diploma. I didn't have a tie, and asked Mom to get me one of Dad's. She fusheled around for that, and Dad popped another T.

David was all dressed up for town, but mom lost track of him and he lost track of the program. He went to the barn to feed Sam again and brush him up. Dad said he was still achy after two killers, but he showed me how to tie the tie. David came in with muddy shoes and straw in his jacket and smelling like horse. It was time to hit it. Dad was really hurting. He tried to stand up and get his walker, but it was no go.

'Sorry, son, it's seized up solid and the foot's burning like hell.'

Mom hadn't started getting ready till everybody else was on track. She came out in her powder-blue suit and dark blue hat and saw what was happening. 'Stay with David, dear. Adam and I will be fine. Gilligan is on now; he'll be ok with that. Here's the clicker. Where are the keys?' How could she remember when the 'Gilligan's Island' was on? Dad nodded, and set the recliner back.

We went out, got sitting in the Datsun, and I turned the key. Nothing; not even a click of the starter. Yet again. There was no need for words: we both knew the drill.

I started the truck and went around to the passenger door to help Mom up. I went to school for the last time and left with a diploma in a leather folder. I assume that's what's in there, anyway. I gave it to Mom before I sat back down in the auditorium and haven't seen it since.

A week later Monday dad was scheduled to go into the clinic. David lost Sam's brush. Mon sent him out to look again and me to help, but we couldn't find it, and he moped. Mom got him to help with the weeding and told me to get a brush and a bag of feed while Dad was at his appointment. Dad got up from the chair and outside with his walker, but when he tried to bend his hip to get in the truck he just stopped, suddenly, and grimaced. I helped him back down and he walkered himself back inside. We called the office to cancel, and Mom explained how bad it was. 'He really can't move around at all, Shirley. Hardly at all any more. How much longer is the wait?'

I got Dad a T-3, and Mom came back into the den.

'You may as well go in anyway, Adam. They'll call the prescription in for you to pick up. Shirley says they have you for the replacement in nine weeks, dear. For the foot operation maybe longer.' She turned to me. '... and we need shampoo and cat food, too.'

Traffic was moving slow in town, so there was lots of time to check out the scene as we all inched along together. Aunt Dorrie holding the door for an old guy in a motorized chair going into the bank, the Sunoco all snowfenced-up while they dug out for the new tanks, and a block ahead a familiar shape sitting on the planter in front of Tim Hortons, having a smoke. Six-three, one-forty, all pointy elbows and knees, and blond dreads held in at the ends by a floppy knit green-and-orange toque in July—that could only be JC. He waved me down with a peace sign as I pulled up at the light, and shouted at the open window. 'My man Adam. Que pas?' He said my name in a way that made it almost rhyme.

I waved back. 'Mr Matchstick.'

There was no rush to get home; I pulled in to the lot and cut the engine.

He'd just started a job laying patio stones for McGuire's Gardens; he was there waiting for Terry to pick him up. 'OK bucks; you working yet?' I said always, but not for pay; with dad out of action I was busy keeping the house running. JC said things must be tight. 'Your mom working?'

'Cutting hair for my aunt; and in the garden. Applied to Sears, but they've only got nights.'

He was looking past me, out at the street. 'Bummer. Call Terry maybe? Your cousin's hot, man; what's her name? There's way more work than we can handle, and he took a serious divot out of his thumb last week. Can't run the saw right with the splint. Can't run it for shit even with his hand regular, actually.'

It took a minute to sort that all out, and at the end of the process, I turned around to see which cousin he meant. Steph it was, waiting for the light in a little Neon, twinkling her fingers at us. Repainted, for sure, Coke can red, and just about as built to last. I turned back to JC. 'Stephanie', and it came to me how upset it got David when she and Amanda were around and they giggled and talked a way that made mom frown and David run around the room and into the walls. JC kept looking. 'I'm in lo-ove. How'd she manage to get the new wheels?'

My not-really-an-answer popped out and my own voice sounded funny to me. 'How'd she even manage to get a license? She can hardly ride a bike.'

JC kept looking past me when he spoke, and Steph must still have been waving, since he did too and spoke without looking.

'...Adam, my brother, reconsider yourself. License is nothing,...just a tiny timbit. That little red wheelie, and curly blond hair—they're the maple glazed and a double-double....'

I was going to say something about the blond hair part, but it got tangled up on itself instead of coming out in words, and while I watched that happen he was working out the rest of his thought. He started to speak and I halfway saw it coming and got a bad feeling, but I'd started it, and had to let him finish. '...and I do plan to roll up that rim to win.'

There was too much to do at home to do anything about calling Terry that week, but we did eventually get caught up. Mom said the chickens were too much trouble, and nobody came by just for eggs any more. 'I hate those stinky birds anyway. More than Dorrie and almost as much as Fred. He'll maybe take them to kill, I guess.' She got David well focused on the tv, and we got to work. I killed 3 for us, and her brother came and caged up the rest and slid them onto the piece of aspenite which he called the bed-liner of his Cheyenne. The gate fell open as he backed out, but he kept going and the chickens made their racket. Good riddance. Mom got ours plucked and in the freezer, and David came in holding a wrecked cage in one hand and a nearly dead bird, by the feet, in the other. Both were a sorry sight, each in its own way. 'I found her by the road.'

Mom sighed, and hustled the wreckage into a garbage bag. 'Fred's likely to leave free chickens for every needy family between here and Point Petre.'

Dad had another appointment on Friday. He said he was feeling better, but we didn't think he could get up into the cab. David and I got the sofa from the den and set it behind the truck. Dad got that far with his walker, and we arranged the cushions and got him to lie down. David and I lifted him up into the bed of the truck, shoved the sofa to the front and wedged it in place with firelogs, and closed the gate. It was a warm July morning, and Dad was feeling comfortable and clever. 'Bungee me in tight, son, or we'll get busted for no seatbelt.'

Off we all went, and reversed the process at the clinic. Doctor Henderson renewed the painkiller scrip, and said Dad was looking close to fine. 'Stay inside and eat junk food, Don. Maybe take a drink. I told them to put you at the top of the list. If you show up in Kingston looking this chipper, they'll bump both of us back down their lists.'

Dad claimed he used to beat up little Georgie Henderson up in grade school 'on the few days he wasn't home with the sniffles.' Doctor Henderson and I helped him up off the table and got him standing in his walker. He started right out of the office. 'Give me some advice I need a doctor for. If they want to know how much it hurts, they can just try to sit me down quick. The folks who measure earthquakes can print out how chipper I sound and how hard the building shakes when they try it.'

That afternoon Dad had his nap and Mom cooked, and I got David set up to wash the truck. I went upstairs to call Terry. For some reason, I didn't want to do it with everybody listening. I got the machine and left a message.

Terry called back on Sunday. He still needed somebody, and told me the cottage where they were working and said come by tomorrow. With a date set, I told Mom, and she said it would be ok to take the pickup.

They were doing a patio on Eastebrook Rd. Terry had a sweet black one-ton Silverado with all kinds of lights and chrome bolted on, and a custom gunrack in back. It looked more decked out for jack-lighting deer than doing landscaping. All the landscaping gear was stored in a trailer with lots of locks and half the air let out of the tires. He shook my hand with his not-bandaged left one and gestured with the other. '...why we need you, Adam. Done any landscaping?' I didn't actually know where landscaping started and yardwork ended.

'Cut the grass, grade the driveway, weed....'

'Can you run the saw?' It was a gas-powered deal with a masonry grinder wheel. Terry handed it to me and told JC to mark a stone and bring it over. 'Fire it up and run the wheel along JC's line. Ease it in till she snaps. Thing's got a kick; hold it steady.'

It looked like an old fashioned chainsaw but without the bar. I set the choke and flipped the switch to start, and braced the body of the engine against my knee and gave the cord a yank. It caught, smoked black, and quit. I backed the choke off halfway and gave it a couple quick little pulls. It fired up: loud, smoky, and smelly. I cut the choke and ran the wheel along the line a few times and the stone snapped. Terry made a sideways motion with his hand laid flat. I flicked the stop, and handed the saw back. 'Your mix is heavy.'

Terry didn't look like he cared about his mix or much else. 'Mix it however you want. Job pays fifteen, cash on Friday, and give JC a ride.' I hadn't negotiated anything before, but it came easy.

'If Dad lets me use the truck I have to get the gas paid.' He was already walking over to pick the next stone off the skid. 'Whatever. We start at 8 and go till we're done.' And that was that for the next few months.

One Friday near the end of September we wrapped up a job by lunchtime, and Terry said let's bag it for the weekend. I dropped JC off at Coach's, and went on home. Aunt Dorrie's K-car was parked in the driveway, and David was soaping it down. I pulled the truck off to the side so she could get out, and complimented David on his technique. He looked pleased. 'It's got to look good as Toronto for Auntie Dee.'

I kicked off my Grebs in the mudroom, and could smell cigarettes and perfume even from there. When I opened the door and went into the kitchen, Aunt Dorrie was sitting at the table talking to mom, and I caught the tail of a sentence before they looked up and broke off talking: '...up like a smashed watermelon....'

They both were caught up in their conversation, and not expecting me. Mom looked at her sister and then me. 'You're home early. Is everything ok?' Aunt Dorrie's sort-of crossed eyes went blank, and she worked on the wing-tip points of her glasses with her index fingers. I nodded, and went on into the house, wondering what they had to talk about that David shouldn't hear.

I thought I'd ask dad, but he was asleep in the lazy-boy with the T-3 jar on the side table next to him. I got cleaned up and went back down, and sat next to dad, who was still sleeping. I tried to be quiet; codine naps were the best rest he was getting by now. I looked at the bottle and thought I should remember to pick up a refill tomorrow, and mom put her head in the doorway and whispered. 'Adam.'

I went in the kitchen, where Aunt Dorrie was stubbing out a butt on a saucer, and I noticed her hand was shaking. Mon looked out the window at David before she turned to me. 'Do you think Dee's car is safe to go to Toronto?'

I tried to think while mom looked and talked. That bag of bones wouldn't last a kilometer on the 401 except as part of a load of scrap metal. 'She has to go and get Amanda. Get, ...bring her home. Tomorrow, ...'

She started to say more, but Aunt Dorrie spoke first, and all in a nervous rush. 'She saw a boy jump onto the subway tracks. Right in front of her. The police brought her home. To her apartment. Her roommate called me last night ...she won't go out of the house; won't talk to anybody, hasn't eaten...just lies in bed, and...' Mom was looking over at me while Aunt Dorrie talked, and I nodded and tried to look thoughtful. I got up and went into the den to ask dad what to say, but he was still napping. Dad usually found an outdoor job to do when Aunt Dorrie came by, and complained about her perfume. '...house smells like pickled beets.'

What could he do now? I watched him sleep for a minute, and went back out to the kitchen. 'Let me take a look at it.'

David was drying the hood off with a rag. 'Hop in, buddy. Let's see if this baby rides as nice as she looks.'

I backed out the driveway, and when I hit the brakes to check for cars on the road, the pedal went right down to the floor. Brake fluid for starters, but even that might not cut it. David angled his head out the window like a dog, and I turned up towards Miller's. Even at low speed, the front bearings whined, and the steering had lots of slop.

All the doors were open at the garage, and there were cars in every bay and more parked in the lot waiting. Cory had Becker's half ton on the lift in the middle bay, and was trying to get the barely there tail pipe off the rusty muffler without too much damage—squeeze a few more months of life out of the old thing. I walked up beside him, and mimed grabbing the muffler and twisting it off its ties. 'Rip it out now, amigo, and save him the gas and trouble of coming back next week.' He laughed, almost. The same half-laugh and way of talking as his father. 'You could have a brilliant future in auto mechanics, Adam.' Pause. 'Just not in the County.' Pause. 'What's up?'

'Do you guys have a car that will make it to the smoke tomorrow? And back.'

He pointed to the window that looked into the office, where his dad had his nose in a filing cabinet. 'Talk to the boss.'

I did, and Mr Miller said he had a K-Car that was in '...way better shape than Dorrie's. It would make it there fine. What does she want to go to Toronto for?'

I wasn't sure how much to say. 'It's a long story. She wants Amanda to come home. I think she bit off more than she could chew with going to art college and living in town. She's worried. My aunt, I mean.'

Mr Miller didn't say anything at first, and looked away and rolled his pen between his thumb and index finger. 'I guess I could put the dealer plates on it.' He swiveled his chair around to be facing the file cabinet, and opened a drawer. 'I have insurance, and wear and tear for five hundred k....'

I wanted to say that it wasn't that long a trip, but I took a breath in and something else came out. 'It's pretty important.'

I looked through the window and back into the garage to where David had come in and Cory was pointing at the underside of Becker's pickup. 'Maybe we could work something out?'

He wheeled his chair around so that he was facing me, but his face stayed blank. 'Maybe so, son. We're backed way up here, and I was hoping to take care of the oil changes tomorrow....'

'Start at 8?' Dad said seal a good deal fast before they think of something else to complicate matters.

He nodded, and waited, and nodded again. 'She's ok? Mandy...? It seems sudden....'

'I think Toronto was just too much for her.'

'Wouldn't be the first.' He rolled the pen.

Neither of us said anything, and he nodded. 'See you at 8, then...'

I went back into the garage, and saw David standing under Becker's truck, holding up a length of tailpipe in one hand and bracing the rotted out old muffler with the other, and the compressor tank filling up drowned out any other noise. Cory waited till it cut off. 'Hold it right there while I get a red robbie....'

David hummed and smiled while we got Becker's exhaust put back together and topped up Aunt Dot's brake fluid. As we pulled out of the lot, he put one hand out the window and reached the other one up against the roof of the car, and sang; softly, and right on key. 'When the red-red robin comes bob-bob bobbin'....'

I hummed along, to myself, '...bob-bob bobbin' ....' When he got to the part Mom sometimes sang to him to get him out of bed in the morning, back when she sang, he changed to a perfect imitation of her clear, sweet singing voice, and carried on without missing a beat, but at full volume. '...wake up, wake up, sleepy-head ....'

Red, red, and I remembered '...a smashed watermelon.' The maples along the road were turning, red and green, and the sun came through in places—shit! -and made a pattern on the milkweed and red sumac and David's song filled the car. '...we'll be hap hap happy-a, hap, hap, happy again.'

Back home I told Aunt Dot that Mr. Miller would lend her a car for the trip, '...just go there tomorrow morning.' We watched her turn the K-car around so she could go out the driveway frontward, and I couldn't stop thinking red, red, ...

By October the mornings were getting brisk for an 8 o'clock start, and Terry was knocking off early. He said he'd drawn a moose tag, so it was no surprise when he said we'd be winding down. The treeplanting gig we were doing would wrap it up for this season. Two days later we were all home for lunch and the phone rang just as we finished. Mom got it, and we heard her listen and say '...that's great Shirley...no, I'll tell him...bye.' She came back in the dining room. 'Lace your skates up, Donny. KGH had a cancellation, and you're booked in for tomorrow morning.' It was too cold to ride in the back of the truck by then, even just into town, so we had to do some headscratching to come up with a plan for the trip to Kingston. Dad's idea was the best, but '...it only adds indignity to my list of hurts.'

Mom tried to head this talk off by standing. 'Help me clear off, David, please...', but dad wasn't paying any attention to her look. 'Isn't this just a wasp in my shorts? I said I'd never ride in that lemon again, and I figured selling it to Fred made it a sure thing I'd never even see it again. In one piece, anyway, and now this...' Mom was already in the doorway, but he carried on. '...never seen that fifty bucks, either, and...'

Mom called her brother and said we needed the car, and could we come over and get it now?

She joked about it while we drove down in the Datsun. 'It does gall your father no end that Fred got the radiator in that big car to work.' She imitated dad's voice. 'Not only can he walk and I can't, but the one damn thing he's fixed in donkey's years is the something I didn't.'

I didn't tell her that Cory said he heard his dad say that the rad from the Eldorado at the far end of the third row had got away, and he thought it was Fred who'd likely helped it out over the fence.

We got to Uncle Fred's and parked beside the Ninety-Eight. Mom went in to get the key, and I admired the big red Olds. I heard his cackly little laugh, and they both came out onto the porch. He waved at me and spoke to mom. 'Haven't had a chance to get that starter motor in yet, Alma...just thinking of doing that tomorrow, first thing, but I guess I'll have to wait on you now...lots to do around here....'

He made a funny face that looked like a grin at first, but then twisted his lips into a crooked line that reminded me more of a coyote than a smile. Mom took a breath, and I thought she was going to say something, but then she stopped short and looked away, at the sky and the overgrown yard, and turned back. Her face was settled now, and she wondered what we'd do, then, Fredrick?

He came over to the Ninety-Eight, turned, and reached in the open front driver's side window. With his back to her, gave me a big wink. He took a slot driver off the front seat, and motioned, with a single wave of the tool, first to me and then on to the hood. '…pop 'er up, Adam.' The smile said he knew that I knew to lean on the hood and reach in under the grill to release the latch, and I caught myself smiling back at him as it squeaked open. He bent in, unscrewed the air filter cover, and stuck a bic in the choke plate to hold it open, and pointed, with the screwdriver, to the driver's seat. 'Hop in there, lad; help a man out.'

He flipped the driver up in the air and spinning itself around, caught it by the handle and leaned over onto the engine so that his feet were sticking up in the air behind him. I heard a click-click, and knew that he'd shorted out the solanoid. He reached around and knocked on the hood with his free hand and made a 'go, go' sign to me as it caught. I mashed the throttle and the motor revved up: we were running. I looked over at mom frowning and watching and followed her eyes to what they were aimed on. Uncle Fred's feet, stuck up in the air, had quarter-size holes in the soles of both running shoes, and matching holes in both of his work socks. Little black circles of dirty foot in the centre of it all faced up to the sky before he flipped himself back right side up, took out the pen, and screwed the air filter cover back on.

We decided to leave the Datsun there and drive back together. Mom didn't say anything as we drove along Kelly Rd, and just looked out the window. It was nice and dry in the fields, and Steenburgh, Johnson, and Hofstetter were all out working. Hofstetter's son had a new baler, and the shiny John Deere green shape went slowly along his goldy-brown rows. It slowed down, and shuddered and burped a round bale out the back as we went by. He waved at us, and mom whispered 'Poudy'.

She was still staring out the window, but knew anyway that I was looking puzzled, and looked at me and talked in a normal voice. 'That's what we called him. That's how he said it, anyway. Poudy. Poodle. Fred. Dee wanted a dog, and mom said I'm already sick as a dog, and we can hardly take care of Fredrick; where will we get food for a dog, too? So she decided baby Fred would be her pet,—a little poodle with his curly black hair. She taught him dog tricks. The day before mom died Fred lay down next to her, still as he could be, and Dee came in to see why it was so quiet and he said 'we're playing dead'. Folks told us he took after *his* father, and he might well have, for all anybody will ever know. They said *he* was brought by *his* big sisters, too. Do you know how to start the car the way he did?'

When we got home I took out the front passenger seat and put it on the porch. At six the next morning we got dad on the sofa again and brought it over to just by the back passenger-side door of the Ninety-Eight. I opened it up, and we got dad stretched out on the sofa and eased him lying head first into the back seat and kept on easing till his head popped out the driver's-side front window. From that point we could angle his leg into the space where the front seat was out. David put a milk crate under his foot, I closed all the open doors, and we were set. Mom opened the back door and leaned down and kissed him good-by, and she revved the engine while I jumped it started. I got out, closed everything back up, and David waved with both arms while we backed out the driveway.

Dad was quiet for the whole drive to Kingston. At the hospital, two black guys brought out a trolley to the emergency entrance, and wheeled him in. The big white clock in the main room said eight-ten. I could tell he was hurting, but he managed a nod and a grimace-y smile: ready to go.

Two women in light green jumpsuits came in with another trolley which looked just like the one dad was sitting on already, and pulled it up next to him. 'Hop over next door, sir. And we need you to lie still. On this one; it's for the OR.' They were wearing headscarves, and had dust-masks tied loosely around their necks; all the same mint green. They got him arranged and turned to wheel him away, and it came to me that they looked like they were dressed up for doing bodywork...and in a way that's what it was.

I tried to follow them down the hall and work out a way to tell dad my joke, but they came to a set of doors, and waved me back.

'Sorry,—sterile only past this door. You'll have to wait out front.'

A young man in the same green uniform came out and held the doors. Dad looked up, saw me and gave a thumbs-up, and they wheeled him in.

I went back to the front desk, and they pointed over to a row of orange plastic chairs, and coffee tables and magazines. 'There's the waiting area.'

'How long will he be?'

'Who?'

As dad sometimes said, the question is the answer. I sat down and started waiting. One of the black guys who had helped get dad out of the car walked by and talked to the guy at the reception desk and went inside. A little while later he came out, saw me still sitting there, and talked to the guy at the desk again. There was a picture of a lighthouse behind the desk, and a smaller clock—ten of ten.

The black guy came over and said something in an accent I didn't understand. I tried to work it out and couldn't. 'Sorry, but...' He repeated himself, slowly and carefully. 'You—have a—long wait—now.'

'How long does it take?'

'Maybe—four hour. Hours. Longer? Maybe.'

He was being nice to me. The floor was a light blue linoleum, with red and white flecks and streaks, and yellow tape marking a centre line in certain places. I didn't know what to say. The direction of the streaks ran past him and over to the swinging entry doors.

He made a 'get up' motion, and spoke slowly again. 'Come this way.'

We walked over to the reception desk, and he spoke with his normal accent, fast, to the guy there. A nurse came in and called him away, and I was left looking at the receptionist guy, who looked at his binder and then me.

'Got it now. Mr Ostrander was a sub-in. He's a relative?'

I nodded as he carried on. 'So the doctor wouldn't have had an opportunity to prep your family.' He saw I didn't exactly get it. 'Talk to them, to you, about what's involved ...in the procedure?' He waved at somebody passing behind us as I shook my head and he kept talking.

'It's a routine procedure. Performance time is usually about two hours if there are no complications. And two or three hours under observation. Post-op.'

I saw a little version of myself and the flouresent light fixture reflected in his glasses, and him looking at me looking. His face changed, and I looked away.

'It's a routine operation, and there's really no reason to worry. There's nothing you can do right now.' The entry doors opened and the black guys were wheeling another patient in. 'It's not very cheerful in here.... Go for a walk, come back around 3, and we'll check. Maybe you can see him then.'

The air felt different, and better, as soon as I got outside. I went down to the water, and walked away from downtown, along a path on the beach.

It ended at a lovely old house with a big lawn, and past that was the jail.

I imagined somebody in a cell looking out over the coils of razor wire at that lawn and the lake. I turned up a street, walked to a bank where the clock said five after twelve, and walked back down and was in front of the hospital again.

Still three hours to go.

I walked toward downtown on a road running along the harbour. On the land side there was a park with huge old maples and red oaks, some timber flowerbeds, and a well-tended lawn. I thought of Terry off moose hunting and how many hours he would have estimated for the contract of maintaining this park. People sat on the grass, and played Frisbee; some were reading. 'Queens', I thought, where Jennica was pre-med. She brought her own frog into biology so she could do an extra dissection;

stuck a pushpin in where she said its heart was when Mr. Parkin said it had to be dead first. Would she recognize me here if she saw me walking by?

Past the park I came to an old limestone building with a new red neon sign over the big black double front doors opening onto a concrete front porch. The word 'Choppers', and a picture of a girl riding the letters like a bronco and waving one arm flashed on and off. There were a few bikes parked out front, and a smell of french fries in the fall air. Lunch seemed like a good idea.

I looked at the row of bikes as I turned to go in. One of them was a black Suzuki 800 with some nice little touches. Half size chrome muffler—that machine would sound great—rough and authoritative. Custom work on the handlebars, too—they swooped up and out and then back down to the grips, which were soft black perforated leather, stretched tight over the controls. I took a close look at the detailing. Beauty ....

'Like that leather look, sailor?' A girl and two guys had just come out the door, and she was looking right at me with a little smile. One of they guys was definitely not smiling, and I looked over at him. He looked past me and out to the street. 'Step back, Jack.'

I did, and wondered why Jack? 'I was...'

He didn't move forward or look at me. 'Whatever you were, don't. Don't look. Don't touch. Don't nothing but keep walking.' The other guy went back in. The girl's eyes were wide and blank, and she wasn't dressed for fall riding. I turned back to the street and kept walking toward downtown.

I got my fries from a cart on the street. Past downtown I saw a boat pull in, and then the sign outside the dock saying it was the Wolfe Island Ferry. I put the fries container in the wastebasket and walked over and read the sign with the schedule and the rates for cars, trucks, semis and so on. At the bottom, in small letters, it said 'Pedestrians and Cyclists—free'.

I could just make out some land over the water, and looked out over the old fort on the left and some clouds coming in on the right, and it all seemed open and light.

I walked over and up the ramp, past a guy in a uniform eating a banana. I slowed up, and thought that he would tell me to do something, but he just finished his banana and threw the peel in the water. Cars came on, and some cyclists. Guys released heavy yellow ropes, a horn blew, deep, and we were off. The air moving around me felt great, and I walked around the deck and up to the front and looked out and down at the shapes of the water being pushed up and into froth by the nose of the boat.

There were people sitting on slatted wooden benches bolted to the deck, and some bicycles leaning against the side rail where I was standing. The one nearest me was a girl's bike with a fitting over the back wheel which held a pair of canvas saddlebags. I looked at this for a minute, and then down at the gear mechanism by the pedals. There were two sprockets, and a lever which picked up the chain and could toggle it from one to the other. The lever ran from a length of stranded wire back to the handles. I looked up and moved a few steps toward the front. The land -which had to be Wolfe Island- was coming into shape, but still blurry in the distance.

A girl in a patterned sweater was sitting and reading on one of the benches next to where I walked up to. She looked up, and the wind caught her hair, and blew it over her face. She put her book down on the bench, reached behind her head and took off a red elastic thing. It struck me that I'd seen girls use these things hundreds of times and didn't know the name for them. I even knew what she'd do next: she put the elastic between her lips, took her hair from inside her sweater collar with one hand and from off her forehead with the other, and gathered the two in a ponytail. She held the ponytail with one hand, took the elastic with the other and made a double twist around the ponytail, and gave her head a little shake. Her hair was light brown, and she looked up and smiled at me watching. She tucked the ponytail back in her sweater collar and looked at me. 'Hi.'

I felt embarrassed, and so I looked at her bike before I looked back at her. 'Hi.'

'It's just a regular old bike. What do you see?'

'I was looking at how the gears change at the sprocket there....'

'Oh. Well, actually they don't there. I'm not sure why.'

I bent down and looked a little closer. I tried to force the lever, but it was locked up. 'It's all rusted. You probably just need to lubricate it.'

'How would a person do that? WD 40?'

The breeze smelled of something I didn't recognize, and I remembered what Mr A used to say and how his high voice echoed in the big auto shop.

Now he was dead. 'WD 40 is just a water diverter. Their fortieth try at cooking up the right formula. You just need to keep some machine oil on it and it should work fine.'

'Machine oil? That sounds pretty industrial for a bike.'

'Or just 3-in-1. Comes in a little squirter can with a red stopper. From the hardware store.'

She smiled. 'Little squirter can sounds do-able. Thanks. You'd be a handy guy to know.'

I looked at the island getting bigger now, and could see a fuzzy treeline and a grey shape where the ferry could dock on that side.

The wind blew some of her hair out of her sweater collar, and she tucked it back in and turned back to face me. 'Do you live on the island?'

It hadn't occurred to me that people did. 'No; we live in the County. My dad is here for an operation.' It came to me as I spoke that I wasn't answering her question. 'I drove him.' She had a red patch on her neck;

the roll-over neck on her sweater didn't quite cover it up. I looked at it and realized that it was a birthmark.

She looked at me looking, and smiled again. 'What operation?'

Nobody had ever given it an exact name. 'They're changing his hip. He's been bad for a while now. His hip for a while, I mean. It's a routine procedure;...the operation. Sorry. I mean I can't explain it very well.'

She got up and stood by the rail. Next to me. Not close to me, but we were looking at the same landscape coming into view.

The water was choppy, and little sailboats were headed out to the open water. There was a smell of fish, and then a breeze and it was gone. I hadn't talked about this, or even really thought about it. 'He can't work, and definitely doesn't like sitting around the house.'

'What does he do?'

'Almost whatever needs to get done. Or used to. Now he's been pretty grumpy. It makes everything different. He gets upset for no reason....' I felt like I should apologize, but she broke in. 'You'd think he would. Considering.'

'Considering?'

I started to work on the answer as she spoke. 'I mean, he'd be completely disempowered? If he saw himself as competent, in-charge, a provider,...and then he becomes a dependent....'

The boat was getting close to shore, and the trees and houses on the island came into focus. The air was fresh, with a clean smell I didn't know.

I'd got the Sierra, driven dad here and would take him home. 'disempowered'... 'dependent' The boat banged against the truck tires hanging on the side of its dock, and shook me out the daydream where I was repeating those words to myself.

She looked and smiled at me as she took her bike and turned it around to face the ramp off the boat, where people and cars were lined up waiting.

'I'm Rachael.'

There was a stone building with big windows and a red steel roof on the shore. She had brown hair and brown eyes. I looked down at that scene from a million miles high, and the boat horn sounded and I floated down and thought of what to say.

'I'm Adam.'

She took her right hand off the handlebar, leaned the bike a little against herself, and reached out to me with a handshake gesture. 'Nice meeting you, Adam.' I shook her hand. 'I hope your father is ok.' It was soft, with stubby little fingers, and fit almost completely inside mine.

She put her hands back on the handlebars, and I wanted to say something to her. '3-in-1'.

She smiled, '...right', and walked her bike down the ramp and off the boat and was reflected in the big windows as she passed them. She got on her bike and rode away. Cars clanged on the steel ramp as they drove onto the ferry deck. I watched the willows she'd ridden past shake in the breeze off the water.

When the ferry got to the mainland, I walked back to the hospital, through the groups of Queen's students talking and playing and reading in the park. Somebody was sitting on an old cannon and playing a guitar, and the big trees were half bare and half leafed. I walked and looked up through them, and it happened for the first time I can remember. The scene went quiet and the sound of her voice flowed in and filled the park, right up to the tops of the maples, and ran over. She smiled and said 'I'm Rachael.' A silent frisbee went by. Her hand was small and soft. A little bell rang. That's what it would be like to have a girlfriend. The bell rang again, louder, and two guys on bicycles, talking and riding fast, moved apart to go around me. I walked on, back to the hospital, and went in.

There was a heavyset man at the front desk now. His hair was white but I couldn't tell if he was young or old. He sent me down a hall to another desk where they went called a nurse to come and talk to me. I waited.

Eventually she found me, and said the operation had gone well. 'Your father is in room 311...' and yes, of course I could see him. She pointed in one direction and went off in another.

Dad was in bed, with the back end cranked up so he was half-sitting, half-lying. There was another bed in the room, but it was empty, and I sat on it so I could see him. Maybe it was only being groggy and in a hospital after an operation, but he didn't look like himself. He said he was ok, but his voice didn't sound just right either.

Neither of us said anything for a little while; I knew he'd wait till he was ready. He looked around the room. 'This place gives me the willies, son', which was actually how I felt too. 'It doesn't smell right.' He wrinkled his nose, and thought about it. '...liquid wrench?...or bad meat...like from when Fred ran down that buck in rut.' All I'd smelled at first was something like perfume and laundry soap, but once he said it I could smell it there too, under the cleaners, and there was no way to get the gamey tang out from up my nose.

'No way I can sleep here. See if you can ask them to let me out.'

I got a nurse, who got a doctor, who got another one, and they talked and ended up sending us home that night. The same black guys wheeled him out, got him in the car, and set him up in the back seat. They helped me jump it started, and we headed home. Me for supper and dad for bed. When he seemed to be sleeping soundly, we went back into the kitchen.

Mom asked with a look, and all I could tell her was that it was a routine procedure, and they said it was successful. She didn't say anything or do anything, or even seem to be looking at anything.

The next morning I bolted the seat of the Ninety-Eight back in place. It rode low in the water, but still smooth, and I had an idea. I got the starter motor from Cory's Regal out of the drive shed, and bolted that in too, and wired it up. Dad still had one of the keys for it in a jar of old keys, and I drove it down to Uncle Fred's.

The house was wide open and the front door swung and slapped in the wind. I realized that I'd never been there alone before, or inside the house, or noticed what a coming-apart-at-every-joint mess the whole operation was. Burdock and jewel-weed had taken over the yard, and the purple and orange flowers made a pattern of coloured dots everywhere. I called Uncle Fred but got no answer, and didn't want to go inside, so I left the key in the ignition and drove the Datsun home.

Mom called KGH, and talked to the surgeon. He told her the same thing I did, but dad was still popping T-3's for the next little while. He had a follow-up a week later, and Dr Henderson told him to think about doing something that wouldn't strain the new joint, and to assume that he wouldn't be doing 'hard, physical work' anytime soon. He stood at the side of his desk in his unbuttoned white coat and stethoscope, and his little gut pinched on the edge of the desktop as he looked down and wrote in the file. Dad bent his leg gingerly just to show he could, and rolled his eyes at me as he got down off the table. 'What's the other kind, Porge?'

Mom was doing some cooking as well as cleaning for the families she worked for, but our bills were more than that brought in. I did chores and errands for the next week, but once we were caught up it wasn't much fun being around the house. Saturday I did the shopping and slowed down at a yard sale on my way back. They were closing up the cottage for the year, and had a not too bad looking orange chainsaw with a '$50 obo—"works"!!' tag on it. I asked why they were selling and the guy said it revved low, and was nothing but trouble. I offered twenty, came home and put the groceries down for Mom, went to the driveshed and wiped off the grease off the saw, and took it into the den to show dad.

'Twenty bucks. What do you think?'

He looked at it for a minute. 'Not much to lose; why so cheap?' I told him and he kept looking. 'Those Huskies are ok, but they're pernickety machines. Your mix has to be right on, and brush off the air filter with a toothbrush if it starts to cut dusty. The exhaust, too.' He tapped a spot on the shroud.

'Right behind there—it just snaps off.'

He kept looking, and smiled. 'But I don't think that's why it's revving low.'

He stretched out his hand, I held the saw, and he tapped the brake forward with his thumb. It made a gentle snapping-into-place sound. 'There you go, son. There's no middle ground for the brake; it's all on or all off. Except here, which is why it's rubbing up against the arbor when she wants to rev up.'

Sunday I went down the lane behind the barn to where the maples had some of their limbs splitting off at the crotch, and bucked up as much of it as was worth the trouble into firewood length. I loaded it up in the manure spreader and drew it out front, and took out a lunker for a splitting block. Even on a cloudy day, I was soon tired and sweaty trying to split it with a maul, and not getting anywhere fast. Roger was sitting on his porch watching, and when he saw me stop for a rest, he limped over across the street. 'Wrong tool for the job, young Adam. A man can die of old age and heartbreak before he splits a cord with that mallet. You go behind my shed and we'll haul the old splitter over, and you'll make tracks. Give me a cord, and we'll both be happy. My woodchooping days are over.'

His splitter was an ugly homemade brute. It rode on an old International wheel-and-axle welded onto the underside of an eight inch I-beam. The stop was a short piece of the same beam tacked on top, and the splitter was a few scraps of flat bar joined to ride roughly along the top chord of the beam. It drove off a scrap of one-inch square stock, ground down to chuck into the take-off of a tractor. All the welds were ugly and drippy, and the wedge was a piece of half inch plate with the leading edge ground down to sort-of, but not quite, sharp. It didn't bite very well. You had to learn to hold the log against the wedge with one hand and cradled against your leg while you reached over to the tractor and eased pressure into the lines with the joystick, and then back the wedge off while you stayed out of the way of the falling split. I got a couple cords split and stacked, and Roger came over and we loaded up his one into the manure spreader and took it back. He still had some wear left in him, and heaved as much as I did. 'Lots of people looking for firewood this winter, Adam. Lots of trees down, too, big ones.'

'Yes sir. We burned five cord last year.' I knew that Dad didn't want to spend on oil if he could help it. 'Can I hang onto the splitter for a while?'

He tilted his hat back, considering, and looked at the ground. 'Course you can, son. Already too much stored at my place.' Which was true, if 'stored' meant whichever way something landed off the back of the truck when your relatives finally got around to returning it.

'Thank you, sir.'

So I was into the firewood business. Dad knew people who needed a few cords, and plenty of neighbours who'd never gotten around to dealing with the downed and half-fallen maples blocking the lanes on their farms; and things took off from there. He was still on T-3 and moving slow, but he said he was on the mend. It definitely lifted his spirits to get on the phone and haggle deals for buying and selling wood, especially with his buddies. 'Nothing like skinning your oldest friends to make a man feel young and spry again.'

These cheapskates didn't care at all about their old maples, and 'fighting trees' was thought to be a proper part of farmer's work. But once Dad called up to make a deal for rights, you would have thought they were selling off the family jewels. We listened from the kitchen while Dad tried to wheel and deal. When he wasn't talking, mom filled in her version of what they were saying, imitating their thin, raspy old hay-dust voices.

'Good heat in those trees, Donny.'

'Limbs mostly down already, Donald. Adam can clear them off in no time.'

David laughed so hard he lay on the floor and cried and said his stomach was breaking. All next week kept asking her to talk like that again.

But the logging went ok, and with more city people building winterized cottages with fireplaces, the market for cut, split, and delivered was good. Then one day I got cocky and tried to plow on through a mudhole in the laneway behind Hofstedder's. The three-quarter ton bottomed out, I tried to find some purchase somewhere with four wheel low, and ended up angry and wheel spinning until the whole thing was sunk in up to the axles. By the time Hofstedder's tractor dragged me out it was the end of the line for the tranny.

The truck looked pretty sad sitting there and we had to use the Datsun the next day to shop. Mr Miller said fourteen hundred to supply and install a new transfer case, maybe more, and both taxes on top. More than I'd cleared in the last two weeks, but there was no firewood business without it. I made some calls and found a case in Colbourne for two hundred cash, but not from a dealer who could just put it in the next NAPA run.

The guy said he'd set it aside, and the next day I headed over. Somewhere around Brighton the weight of the last month lifted itself a little, and I noticed that it was a beautiful late fall day. The leaves were down, and the ochre coloured view opened up the way it does that time of year. I hadn't been alone driving with the windows open on a nice morning since dad's hip went. I heard a rifle crack. Then again, and I thought dad would miss deer season and wondered if Terry got a moose. Who might swap venison for a cord?

Just outside Brighton I could see the lake running all the way out from the marsh to the horizon. The land to my right rolled up from the road, and then rose steeply, facing South. Next to a white house with a fancy old porch was a just-pulled-out orchard with the trees lying there sideways, roots still holding dirt. Dad said apple made the best firewood, with little emerald flecks in the flame and a green-apple smell to the smoke.

I slowed down and pulled over in front of the house and walked up the sloped path and the concrete steps to the porch, opened the storm door and knocked, and looked around while I waited. The house had stucco walls finished in a dog's paw texture, and a fancy doorcase, with the door between a bank of sidelights on each side. The lights had paneled woodwork below and a transom ran over top of it all. One of the sidelights was busted out, and an old checked workshirt was stuck in the hole, with one sleeve hanging down out the front. It looked dark and quiet inside, and I thought 'retired farmer, hard of hearing maybe?' I knocked again, harder.

I was half right. After a minute an old lady answered, pulling the door just a little open and her other hand holding a housecoat tight to her neck, and scowling. 'Yes?'

Scowls make me want to apologize.

'I'm sorry, mam.' I looked over to the orchard, where the uprooted trees still had their apples. She opened the door another few inches.

'I wondered about the orchard, mam. Is that wood spoken for?' We both looked away for a second, and she kept scowling.

'It's not an orchard any more, and I've made an arrangement with a chap to remove the wood. I signed the paper yesterday.'

She didn't close the door, and kept looking up at me. I looked at the apples, gold and red in sunlight, and it came to me what kind they were. 'Did you make a deal for the apples, too, mam, or can I take couple? My mom loves Jonas but you don't come across them very often.'

She opened the door further, and the sun hit her old face looking at mine. 'Hardly ever any more. Do you have a bag to put them in? They are lovely apples.'

She brought me a garbage bag. 'They keep well; take all you want.' I said thanks, took a half bag and carried on and bought the transfer case. Cory's dad let us use the shop on Sunday for thirty-five cash. We changed the case over, and I was back in business. Mom made applesauce and remembered the empires and idas and two jonas at our place when it was her family's place and before they cut down the orchard.

The next night it turned cold,—for good for this year, it felt. I had to set myself to getting out doing firewood, but the saw ran easier in that weather. Dad sharpened the chain and filed down the rakers, and I switched over to a lighter bar oil. Business was better than ever till it snowed. That was December fifth, and the limbs were covered up and it was getting dark and cold early. My hours were getting slack. The cottager's driveways weren't plowed either, and I had to postpone some deliveries and it snowed yet again.

I looked out the window and wondered about other ways to pay the bills. Dad must have been thinking along the same lines. 'If the truck had a plow on, son, I bet we could have made those deliveries and charged them for plowing too.'

The forecast called for snow, snow, and then more. We had wieners and applesauce for lunch and watched the Simpsons with David. Dad remembered that Carl Mitchell used to plow driveways. 'He got hit from the driver's side that time. The truck was totaled, but I think the rig was fine. No way Roger would have sent anything worth saving to Harrison's. The spare from that wreck was still on his back left, last time I saw.' I wasn't sure.

'I think he got new tires last year', and snow fell all night.

Next morning the County cleared roads, and Roger came out to dig out the plowrow at the bottom of his drive. David and I took shovels to do ours, and I mentioned the rig to Roger. It felt funny asking, since he never once said a word about Carl's accident, but he seemed fine. 'Of course, son, we'll go have a look when we finish our chores here.'

It looked ok, and even had all the lines and controls. I offered him a hundred cash. Shoveling must have taken some of the fight out of him. 'A hundred and plow me out if you get it working. Whenever it needs it.' That was too easy; unlike getting it back to where I could work on it. It took the three of us and Roger's loader an hour to break it out of the frozen ground and hump it onto the truck bed.

Cory's dad said we could use the shop again on Sunday. I got the power steering pump from the Regal out of the drive shed, and we hooked it up. Cory got two pieces of three-eights plate from the pile, and we put the truck up on the lift. I rolled the tanks over to underneath, and held the sparker while he put the hood on and tilted the visor up. Without planning it, we both imitated Mr A: 'A before O, or up you go.'

He took the sparker and opened the acetylene. 'Poor guy, getting a death sentence the week you retire.' He tacked the plate to the underside of the frame, sticking out a foot to the front. We unloaded the plow with the hoist and lifted it up clear of the bed, lowered the truck and turned it around and brought the front end up to right below the hanging rig. Cory wrestled it around while I welded it to the plate. We hooked up the hoses and drilled out the firewall to run them through inside. I mounted the sticks on a scrap of ply, and was ready for the snowplowing business.

Two days later it was ready for me. They called for 30 cm and high wind, and the county pulled the plows for the day. Dad got out his book and hit the phone, and I had six driveways for the next morning, plus he'd left some messages that hadn't called back yet when I went out. Dad seemed to know how this business worked, as if it was something well understood by everybody born with any sense to begin with.

'Don't lose any time trying to collect right away, Adam. Just make a list of who you did when, and we'll send them a bill.'

He didn't worry the small stuff like the fact that I'd only rode with him years ago when he did our drive or that I didn't know the places I was going to plow very well. 'How will I know where the drive is with all this snow?' He said just take it careful. 'Keep the blade up a bit, and work your way along piece by piece. Ride the clutch, and use the blade to pull the snow back out into the road when you go. Push the plowrows off on both sides when you leave so it looks wide when they see the job. But not too far; and whatever else you do wrong, don't scrape their precious tress.'

By almost Christmas Dad was feeling pretty good and said this new hip was way better than the one he was born with and he'd like to sign up for the other one now, and not wait on his luck again next time. He'd lined up a few more plowing accounts, and Mom was back to cooking for people who didn't have time to make dinner,—I delivered to some of them, too. We don't usually do many Christmas presents. Dad's family hadn't had much money and the tradition was that each person drew a name of one other family member and made them a present. It was a rule that you tried to use what you had already, and couldn't spend more than a dollar. Mom said those were 'depression dollars', but the tradition held. David asked why Sam wasn't on the gift list, and mom thought fast. 'He's yours, so it's up to you to add his name.'

I must have gone to sleep at some point around thinking that, because I was dreaming of Sam when Gail gave me a gentle shaking, and spoke softly. 'Snoring.' She turned over and pulled up the quilt, and hum-spoke '...raining, it's pouring...'.

Her warmth filled the bed and the night and I looked out the window: it was half-sleep now and four days from Christmas then, both at the same dreamy time. Dad said they were calling for another storm. He thought he'd call the cottagers I plowed to see if they wanted to book getting cleared out if they were planning to come down for the holidays. 'Check the rubber on your blade, son; you've been dragging it hard lately.'

I looked the next morning, and it was nearly down to steel where it bolted in. I called the guy in Colbourne and he said sure come by, he had a good used one if I could unbolt it off the plow. 'Better come now if you do want it—the plow's out in the yard, and you'll be rooting around in a snowdrift if you wait too long.'

Off I went, and remembered the old lady when I passed the stucco house with the cut-down orchard. The driveway wasn't plowed, and her brown Reliant was parked at the top of it with the west side completely drifted over. Out of instinct, I slowed down and wondered if she wanted it plowed out, and saw the shapes of the fallen trees still there, each one banked up on the west with a drift and on top the Jonas still held on, now light brown and frozen and all dotted around the branches and drifts. The light bulb came on: David, Jonas, present for Sam...I stopped, just past the drive, checked the road behind and backed up to the driveway. I put it in four-wheel high, lowered the blade to a few inches, and worked my way up the drive, zigzaging the snow off to each side. The old lady must have heard the noise, because she was standing behind the closed door with a broom when I'd finished and went up the concrete steps. I saw her face in the sidelight next to the hand I was reaching out to knock with. She opened the inside door, and at first didn't recognize me, and scowled the way she had before. I took off my toque, and tried to think of what to say, but then she recognized me, and some life came into her face. 'Back for more apples?'

Yes, I was, if that was ok? 'My brother has an old horse who would think a bag of them was heaven on earth.'

She made an 'of course' shrug. 'Indeed he would. And I'm not expecting anybody, so thank you for plowing, but it's not necessary.'

I got an odd feeling talking to her. She wasn't being friendly or unfriendly, she just stood at the door like she was waiting for me to figure out what I was supposed to do next. I looked over at the circular shapes of apple tree tops and the browny-gold jonas in the snowdrifts and said what came to me. 'That guy didn't come to clear away the firewood?'

Her face clouded over, and she looked away. 'Take all you want. Apples, that is. Do you need a bag again?' She still wasn't looking at me, and made a little sniffling sound, and her eyes were shiny when she looked back up at me. I felt uncomfortable and didn't know what I was looking at but couldn't look away. She kept looking. 'He came, but he didn't clear the trees away. I forbade him.'

She set the broom against the doorframe, and leaned herself against it, and looked down at the rag in the window. I wondered if she'd seen it from the outside before. 'They won't go before I do, cut or standing. Now he's filed in small claims for the value of the firewood.'

She looked up at me, and I thought of David when Smokey ate the mouse. I was embarrassed, and didn't know what you are supposed to do when somebody looks like they might cry. She backed away from the door, and held it open. I looked at the shirt sleeve where it hung loose. 'If you have same tape, I have a piece of cardboard I could cut for your window.' She spoke with pauses between her short sentences.

'Come in, and stand on the mat. It's cold. I'll get your bag. And the tape. I'm very sorry. Yes. Please excuse me.'

I got a scrap of cardboard from the cab and went back inside. She came back, and I cut the piece to fit and taped it neatly to the frame and tried to think of what to say. 'It's too bad about your trees. It must have been a beautiful orchard.'

She took a kleenex out of her sleeve and dabbed the teary eye. When she looked back up at me it was still shiny. 'Yes, it was that. Magnificent, ... and delicious apples.'

I started to say 'they are so', and how much we all liked them, but I saw she wasn't listening. 'That orchard was my wedding present from my grandfather. Capt John Hutcheson, RAF, -gentleman farmer, angler, and nurseryman....' Her voice changed, and she started to do what sounded like an imitation. '...although never the three at one....' She caught herself, paused, and changed back to her own voice.

'He was one of the first growers to develop that cross. Jonagold. He grafted the best branches he could find onto his own root stock when he noticed where things were headed with me and Jack DeMille. He saw that that Jack was the one- saw it well before I did.'

A small smile: '...well before. And for years on afterward he told anybody who'd listen—as well as several he didn't realize were as deaf as he was—how much he enjoyed watching his daughter set the hook. He bought the lot next to Jack's house - this house - and planted the trees while we were on our honeymoon—June 1954. We spent our life together keeping that stand as perfect as it could be, and it rarely felt like work. Every year for Christmas we gave everybody a gallon of cider and a peck of fruit, and we knew that they thought it was the best present anybody could get. Dad and Jack tried to ferment some, but it never amounted to more than vinegar. They were fine the way nature grew them. But they're only good for so many years, like everything else. Now it's just us left, and when they go so will I.' It took a second to work that one out, and then the story was done. 'The colour of jonagold out the kitchen window is all that's left of me.' She looked at me with her shiny eyes. There was an elaborate piece of furniture in the entry where we stood: dark, with a seat, coat hooks, and a mirror. I saw myself in a touque, between 2 old coats. 'More story than you bargained for, young man? Here's your bag.'

Things happen to me. 'I'm no good at bargaining, mam.' I don't know where they come from. 'Maybe I could take some cuttings? My mother knows how to graft. She has some roots we could use.'

Things happen to me. The snow was coming on hard and I got the hand saw from the cab and cut the branches and put them in a garbage bag. I watch them happen, but don't understand or cause them. Then I'm carrying on, dealing with what happened while the next thing builds up somewhere in the distance, moving towards me at its own speed. I made the best suggestion I could think of. 'I could pot up a few of them. It's a long way to fruit, but Dad and my brother need something to do. There used to be an orchard behind our house. Maybe all your grandad's trouble to keep the line going won't be for nothing.'

The storm kept coming, and the next day I plowed, and on Christmas Day it snowed again and we were all inside together. I had David in the draw, and gave him the big garbage bag of apples tied with a red ribbon and a card that said 'David and Sam, from Santa.'

Mon looked pleased with the cuttings. 'Grafting isn't too hard, but you have to be delicate. My hands won't do it any more. You'll have to get tape. I'll show you.'

Sun came in the open window and filled the room with morning and light the colour of Gail's short hair. She gave my shoulders a shake. '...let's motor, amigo. John said first thing.' She hummed a tune which sounded familiar. I could see the row of the boxes up the lane when I looked out the window. '...raining, it's pouring...'

'You managed to sleep through it.'

'Good thing, too; I need my rest. We've got a full plate today.'

We loaded up the boxes and ran them down. John pressed, and his buyer was there with a lovely little stainless tanker by the time we had the boxes loaded back up and tied on the flatbed. He gave us our check and five litres of juice. 'Good apples, Adam. You guys know how to show them the love. ...how's Alma? ...good...say hi from me.'

That night before supper we sat in the den with the fire going, and David's treat was to watch the Adams Family. Gail brought in one of the plastic litre jugs. 'We've got a treat for you, Alma.'

Mom smiled wide, and went to get the blue rimmed cocktail glasses out of the corner cabinet in the living room. 'Let's drink a toast.'

David turned around from the tv we thought he was watching so intently. 'You don't drink toast.'

Mom passed him a glass. 'It's a way of speaking, David. We all think of something together, a wish, or something we'd like, and...and...'

I could tell from the pause, and their faces too, that they were both thinking the same thing, each in their own way. I wondered how to change that, but Gail had it fixed while I was still wondering.

'...or we say thanks to the people who made a good thing happen...'

Mom looked at David. '...and clink our glasses together—gently, like so—and say who we're thanking all together. Then you take a sip.' David seemed to be satisfied with that, and imitated the way she held her glass. She must have been carried away with the occasion to be careless enough to forget the kind of thing we'd all learned so well for so long. 'It's delicious when they've just been crushed.' David's face fell when he heard the word, and then Mom's too. I tried to figure out what to say, and once again was nowhere near started by the time Gail finished. 'It doesn't hurt them. They fall off, and then they grow back next summer.'

Mom raised her glass. 'To the pickers', and we clink-clinked formally, and sipped. The glasses were still cold from being out in the living room, and when the blue rim touched my lips, I could taste...gold, sweet, October...and the apples from the trees I'd planted from the cuttings from Mrs DeMille's orchard that was gone now; from the branches her grandfather had grafted onto the roots he'd grown long before he watched her fall in love; from the fruit we'd crushed that morning: it would grow back next year and years after.

David

Snow is white rain, mud is sweet...soft, and barny.... I open the window to smell....

...*David! What are you doing? It's freezing in / STOP!*
...*stop*...say to myself what I say to them: think how he sees it. A hundred stops!; years of thinks... —To Donny when he yelled at him for banging on the piano.—To Adam when he'd poured brake fluid on the driveway so he could '... watch the green... ',—even to Dorrie when he packed the mud on her car to cover over the rust spots. Stop! To him, it all felt perfectly normal. Though God knows, and Adam said, '... that clunker did need the body work.'

Hold on, I'd tell them, each time, and sharply if necessary,—think for a minute. Anybody else would understand that you're a little heated up, and maybe they shouldn't be doing whatever got you riled. But he's got no fight. He's thinking about colours, or whatever it is he sees. Every harsh word is a punch, and he doesn't have the reflex to fight back. Or even duck. A boy like that needs to know that somebody is always on his side, no matter what. And if not me, who...?

So it's Stop!, Alma, think. Say calmly, quietly: 'David, please, it's quite chilly with the window open like that. What do you see out ...?'

And now, with a winter's worth of slow time to look back on everything—the months that were coming when he said 'white rain', that summer with the damp weather and with Fred, and finally, in the fall, with finding him kneeling in the dirt—I tell myself to think it over. If you're supposed to be the one he can count on, then try to imagine it. How did it all look to David...?

...how it's winter stale in the house, and bright out the windows where we look, two at each. How Gail nods her head. '...starting to turn. There's hope for us all.' How mom looks good blue and brown grass between the grey snow places. Melting.

After dinner we watch 'The Simpsons'. Gail smiles when they talk and drive, and mom goes out to do the dishes. Bart locks Skinner in a little room, and Gail laughs yellow. Keeps laughing and her face gets pink. She puts her hand on Adam's shoulder and laughs.

I look over. 'What's so funny?'

She looks at Adam. 'I'm sorry David.' Mom stands in the doorway with the blue striped drying towel. She holds it up waving when I look over. 'Your turn, David. When your program is done.'

It is done. I stand up and look back at Gail. She's sitting still. 'I just felt like laughing. It's not just 'The Simpsons'. Well, it is a little, but I think almost anything could make me silly at this point. What a winter. We've hardly gone out for five weeks. And now I feel like laughing.'

Her colour is a good yellow. I dry the dishes, and arrange the table things in a line from big to small and the house is quiet. The tv is off and they're gone when I finish. I go back and turn off the lights in the kitchen and look at the quiet while sounds come in to fill it up. The fridge humming up and down...mom's door upstairs...coyotes laughing outside...they mix in till it's full, and I go upstairs; dark and winter and nothing to do.

The next day is warm too, blue like mom when she's blue, and sharp yellow grass in the going out snow. Adam looks out the window after lunch. 'Almost there, folks. Every day in every way....' He stands up, swings his arms, looks. 'Hey David—let's lose the plow today—just to celebrate.'

We dress warm. He starts the rust truck, raises the plowblade up high and drives to in front of the driveshed. Waits. I kick ice away and slide the door open. He comes ahead to just inside. I put my hand up, and he stops, idles, points his glove at the dolly, and I roll it over to under the blade. He thumbs-up, and I go back. He holds his hands sideways, one above the other, and I go in front to the dolly and hold mine that way too...as far apart as the dolly and the blade. He talks loud. 'Ready? Clear?' He watches my hands, and lowers it down, little by little till I clap. He turns off the truck. Adam knows how to work: sockets the nuts off and hands me the cold ones to glove. Striped sun in the shed floor, breeze and he's done. He raises the plow arms, and the blade sits on the dolly by itself. I give him the nuts to twist back, and he points to me to squeeze oil. We wipe it clean and roll it to its summer place, side-by-side push to make it sit rightways in the striped corner. '...and that's that for that,...maybe. Weird weather like lately and we might need it in June, eh bug?'

We put the tools back on the black oil bench shelf and get the pliers. He drives the truck onto the cement behind the barn for summer. He pops the hood, and we unscrew the battery cables. Geese over. He nods. 'There we go. Done like winter...'

I wave good-by, hands crossing overhead, and see him between them looking up the slope to the orchard. 'Go for a look?'

There's a little bank of snow stretched out behind Sam's pink rock. A new cedar came up next to it. I taste the air. Adam is red. We get there and look at the trees with some little brown apples we missed. Lots of snow lines on the slope above and twisted grass and burdock on the house side of the trees.

He walks, picks up sticks. 'What do you think?' Keeps walking, touches his gloves on the branches. I look and wave. No swallows home yet, he snaps a branch, Sam warm and grey then...I'm cold.

Adam looks, touches, walks. Blue shadows on the drifts and 'I'm cold...'. We walk back, down the muddy ice laneway to inside, and the sun comes in the kitchen.

After lunch I do my chores. Firewood, dry dishes, tie the garbage. Nothing to do. I go in the dining room and open the cold piano keys door. Look but don't touch, up and down they run....

It's turns cold that night. Adams makes the fire big. When we come back up, Gail is whispering to mom. I go in the den. Gail and Adam go back in their house. I swing my arms, sit in the lazy-boy, and mom comes in. 'Do you know what's Thursday, David? I shake my head and she talks. 'April 10th?' I remember. 'Adam has a birthday.'

'Um-hm. A special one. He's thirty-nine.' She's very blue. 'David....'

She stops. I wait. She comes over and sits down in the couch instead of telling me what. She's quiet; then talks. 'Do you remember his hair was red and brown and orange all at once? How you said like a pumpkin? When....' She's soft and the Bongard bronze floorlamp shines in her eyes like crying. '...try...but they slip...so fast.' She pulls her sweater around her with her arms. 'Thirty-nine...and you thirty-one...and....'

She sits up straight. 'Gail has a lovely idea for his cake. Will you help me make it when they're in town on Thurday?'

Thirty-nine and thirty-one is older by eight. 'Can we put thirty-nine candles all on a cake?'

'Not exactly, but something nice. I'll show you.'

I sit back in the lazy boy. *Happy birthday to you.* Mom stands up. 'I'm tired now David. I think I'll go up.' She looks down at me. Will you put a little more wood on the fire, please? It's perishingly cold.' I nod, and rock back.

She looks. 'Thank you.' Looks, and her eyes shine. Looks. '...So fast, David....' I stop rocking and sit still. Listen. '...nights I can't make one minute move to the next...' Her blue is very pale. '...then nineteen is thirty-nine and...' I listen, but she's quiet now. '...won't forget the fire...?' I nod. 'Goodnight, David.'

I put two logs in the fire, and wait. It's quiet, and nothing comes in to fill it up. I sit, and wait...nothing.

Thursday Adam and Gail do their errands in town. Mom gets out the recipe box. 'Reach up for the cake pans in the back of the top shelf, please David.' She shows me the recipe. '...and get the things on that list, please?'

We mix and bake. The sun comes around and onto the kitchen and they come back. Adam goes out and Gail stays in. She puts things away and takes three red and green apples out of a white plastic bag. 'Chile's finest.'

Mom gets the card for frosting from the box. 'Ok David. Now for the fun part. Will you get the things for this, please?'

Gail cuts the skins off the apples on the chopping board, and keeps cutting little by little until the apples are as small as our ones are in summer. They sit on the cutting board in a triangle. She puts the yellow paring knife into the stem, and circles the middle part out. Mom makes the frosting up in a silver bowl, and I stir it up till it's hard enough. Gail gets a bottle from the spice rack. 'OK David. I want you to add this, but just a drop at a time. Ready?' I unscrew the top and squirt in a drop, and the frosting turns pink. 'Another.' It turns redder. 'Two more.' It's bright red now. 'Perfect, David, perfect. Do you want to do the cake first?' I know how to spread it on the layers. Gail puts the three little peeled apples on the cake, and turns them around so they're set on the frosting. 'Almost there. Alma, can you get us a few euonymus leaves?...or better yet, with the stem left on a couple inches? Please.' Mom stops, smiles, nods and goes out. Gail takes the spatula, and nudges the apples a little so that the holes she cut are pointing straight up. 'Can you hold the icing bowl right here for me?'

She works slowly, and spatulas frosting all over the apples and pushes little parts around until they look like funny bright red apple shapes. It takes all the frosting we have left, and she gives me the spatula. 'Want the lickings, such as they are?' I lick and watch. She takes nine green candles out a box, and puts them on the cake in a circle. Pushes them with a fork or a finger to make them stand up straight. 'There, almost.' Mom comes in with the dark green leaves, and Gail cuts them so each two leaves have one stem. She pokes it into the frosted apple where the leaf would be on a real one. 'Viola.' Mom smiles and claps, and me too. 'What's viola?'

Gail puts her left hand behind her back and holds her right one out, pointing the knife flatways over the cake, and makes a little bow.

Mom wears her good new sweater for dinner, and makes roast pork with applesauce. Adam and I have seconds. After dinner we sit, and Adam pats his stomach. 'That was delish. I'm set for the next few days.' Gail looks over at mom. 'He thinks we're going to let him off the hook this year. Mom shakes her head. 'Oh, he knows better.' Adam shakes his head, too. 'I guess

I should.' He smiles. '...*brought up to know better*" is my motto. Ok. So let's get it done.'

Gail goes out to the kitchen, and I know what will happen. Mom leans over to me and says what she always says when the cake comes out. 'Just this once...' Adam and I say together '...just this once...' and Mom finishes '...you can be a silly goose. Just this once, and that's it.'

Gail comes in with the red cake and Adam looks at the apples with the candles on fire and the green leaves. Shakes his head and laughs. 'That is too custom....' He looks at mom and Gail holding the cake in both hands and mom looks at me. She nods and Adam talks. 'Ok Mr silly blue goose, your turn. Pipes all warmed up?'

She puts the cake down in front of him, and stands back. I nod, close my eyes, and think frosting, red, and the sounds. Open my eyes, and my singing voice sings. 'Happy birthday to you. You belong in the zoo. You look like a monkey, and you smell like one too.'

They clap, he blows out the candles, and kisses Gail on the cheek.

We eat cake. Two sweet pieces for me. The apples taste white. After we're done, Adam and Gail go back to their house. I want to watch tv, but mom says she's tired and asks me to do the dishes and dry tonight.

Not sleepy. I sit in the lazy boy, rock back and forth. I look at the off tv, and taste red frosting. Gail calls it icing. Happy birthday. I stand up and walk in the empty room, but my sock catches on the floor. Tap my finger on the chilly window. Marching finger feet. Empty room. I go out and open the dining room door, and go in the floor squeaks and turn on the light. The curly chesterfield with a green blanket, the black piano with the round chair, the Bongard bookshelf with the footed bowls in a row. I stand. Hear empty. Wait. Mice, and dusty. Nothing to do. I go up.

The rest of Spring comes, and colours...so many I can't think all their names in one time. Adam and I get our black gum-boots and go to the white flower orchard up the lane in muddy feet; '...have a look.'

Grey Sam is pink now and Adam is a different red in his mussy hair than before and I know the trees won't stay white or smell sharp.... '...clean up some deadwood, buddy?', and we do.

We take the pieces to put with the ones from last year on the wind side. The top of the pile is scraggy up to my waist and pointed geese honker in low, and a snake! I honk too, smell sweet white apple air. Adam looks over, so I tell: 'Snake in the grass.'

He laughs while he works. 'Poor guy probably thinks he's getting attacked by a giant goose!'

I half raise my arms to a blue goose flap, but Gail says no silliness in the orchard and winking red Adam says 'without written permission', and

I stop. Sun *you are my sunshine* the wind blows it through the white trees, and ...'... hey David, check out next door.' I look over past the fallen down poplars and a white pony walks up the Burrit fields are Smith's now to a bale of old hay and sniffs old. I sniff. Adam watches too: the pony bites, chews, and sniffs. He stops watching, goes back to work and I keep watching, small, white, no bridle, long grey neck hair, chewing, smelling *Stewball was a racehorse* watching and *I wish I was mine* until Adam calls in his work voice. 'Come on, we're good.'

I look back and he's going; turn and walk, me too, and *I bet on the bay*. I run to catch up. I remember wind smells, they blew the old branches off, we walk.

The last snow goes. Yellow grass goes green and tulips, red, purple, velvet... they go and sparrows come. Summer sky should come too and we wait but it doesn't. We sit on the porch and watch the rain fall and drip off the roof and run on to away. The chairs sit in a row and Gail stands up, walks to the end of the row. 'There's a lot of waiting in this business.' The colours are dull, their names don't come, and she walks back and sits down again. We're all quiet. The mail car stops at the mailbox, reaches out, flips the flag and drives away. Adam looks back and talks flat. 'You're finally getting the hang of it if when you can't do anything and you can't do nothing, either', and the rain comes hard on the roof and lightning thunders loud, *rain, rain go away*....

'We wait for spring and we wait for summer and we wait for fall ...' Her voice is pointy '... we're never happy with where we are.' Adam turns his head fast looking past me with his voice easy like talking to Sam. 'You've got it. That part. Now forget that it's waiting.'

It thunders again the way Sam doesn't like. Gail gets up and goes in. I stand up and walk around the porch corner to where I can see next door and the white pony with its head in its house and its back out in the rain. The rain comes loud and thunder. It keeps standing there. Adam shouts from behind me. '... have a look at the loader lines? Just in case it ever dries up enough to drive it out.'

I know not to shout. 'Why does he stay out in the rain?' He runs to the driveshed. I run too, and we stand in the door and look over together, past our house and on to the water back pony. 'Just having a shower, amigo, he's probably happy... get me the needle nose, eh?, and the ratchets.' Adam knows and we work. We bleed the dark green bucket line fluid into the white pail, and he pours new, lemon-green back into the line and checks the level. '... a little more, there. See ... right up to the mark ... ?'

We wait and wait. Adam says 'wait, summer will come...' and she stares. '...someday...maybe...my prince....'

I move the table for us to have lunch on the porch. Mom is blue arranging things to right for how they look. 'David give me the napkins please and thank you,' and Gail comes last. She walks light on the grey porch floor boards, 'Alma this is lovely, and your garden...', sits down, '...sorry to keep you hungry folks waiting...' and we start lunch. Adam shoos away flies and we watch the clouds in quiet.

A bee lands on my plate and I hiss it. They've got the wrong colour relish out and my porch chair doesn't fit and I try different places. Nothing is smooth and the chair scrapes. Mom looks at me. 'Try to be more still please David. Have some potato salad?, ...are you alright?' There's a nest in the ceiling...flies but no birds.

Gail is being shy. *My my shoefly pie.* We sit still after lunch and watch the grey sky roll along over itself. Adam says '...calling for rain, rain and more rain.' Gail keeps being shy and she stands up and turns around. 'I think we should think about spraying.'

Mom and I do the dishes and they walk up the lane to look. They come back when we finish. They're sad, and mom looks '...Well?'

Adam shakes his head. Quiet. '...so damp...' No colour. 'Think of a pest, and we've got it...tent caterpillars, rusty leaves blight, poppy fungus...some black things we don't know....'

Gail walks away while they talk, back out to their house. Mom sits down. 'I remember when Donny's dad had the tent-pillars. That was a wet summer, too.' She nods. 'We burned them off with a plumbing torch...' She looks at me. '...still got some good fruit that year, I think. A little watery...' She looks at Adam looking out the kitchen window. 'What do you think?'

He bends down a little to see around the hydrangea. 'Something running around out there?' His voice sparrows up and down. '...Prince... after a squirrel or something; cheese friggin Lousie...can't Roger keep track ...?' Mom gets blue and still, looks at him. 'What do you think?'

He's still bent down to window looking. His voice darts more. '...talk to Roger, maybe.' She looks, looks at me, back at Adam. 'What do you think?'

He turns around, out of the window, looks at mom...'Ok, Ok. I think apples don't grow in a damn rainforest...' and back out the window and '... why can't Roger...?' stops, looks down. '...Gail does the thinking.'

Mom sits still. He turns back to face into the kitchen. '...And she's probably online now and knows half of everything about fungus and blight...'

Mom sits just sits. ' ...but I know that we'll have to spray.' He folds his arms and stands still and his voice is low. 'There, I said it.'

Mom sits soft and blue, next to me and looks over. 'David and I are both tired. I'm very tired. Would you hang the laundry, please and we need to go shopping. While Gail thinks and I rest.' He fixes his voice with a word-laugh, and goes out. We sit quiet in the empty kitchen. Her eyes are half closed.

Everything is fast and shiny next morning. Gail drinks coffee and looks outside and eats toast standing up while we sit. The colours are bright and right. Wind blows through the open house, and Adam stands up and takes the plates and cups away. I stand and mom sits. 'Finish your toast David. Sitting, at the table please.'

He's red, stands still, takes a breath. 'We won't start without you, bud...' turns around '...and for sure we won't start at all till the wind drops. I hear airbrakes...a truck on the road. Stopping here, and I stand up again. I hear the engine, and look out the window. Adam is backing the tractor out of the drive shed. I run out. He swings it around to go out the driveway frontwards, and he stops, cuts the engine. 'Ok, you're here: we can start.' He points to the truck at the foot of the drive. 'We just have to hook up the tank.'

I hop on the back and we ride down the driveway. A yellow man with a red hat I don't know gets out of the truck with a paper. 'Morning, Adam.' He takes the paper and his truck stays bumpy running and I can't hear some words. '...Bill...doing...?'

He gets off and they talk. '...mix she said you want...' He unhooks his hitch, talks. '...no, not much of a one, so far, but your timing is good now. Two clear days for this part, ...rain for the weekend ...wash it back off ...'

They unhook a red tank from his truck. Adam comes back and we ride the tractor to back up to the red tank with hoses and pipes. The man looks, talks quiet. 'I'm just in the way here...see you five or so...hi to Alma...' Adam shines red in the sun but the tank is old red and the truck drives away. 'Spot me, David, eh...?' He backs the tractor to under the hitch, just right. I hold up my hand to say stop. He comes over, winds the handle to down on the ball. He flips the lock over and taps it down hard with his foot. We drive the tank up the driveway.

Gail is on the porch, white all over, and she puts a white winter hat on her face and white gloves. Adam cuts the engine and goes in his house. I hear the kitchen windows close and he comes out. He's white now too. '... ready to do or die, if not both.' His voice is sad, and Gail talks wrong too with the hat down on her face. 'Buck up, dear', and he smiles crooked. She looks at me, ...Adam does too. 'Stay here, bud, ...and actually inside for this morning would be good. We have to give the trees some medicine, but it's not good for you. Pretty bad, actually. I'll tell you the story later.'

His voice is right but dark. I'm jumpy and try to remember what that dark means. I can't learn and then they're gone up the lane to the orchard.

Tomorrow is sunny again and the colours are right when I come down and mom is blue in the kitchen but when they come in the colour goes away. Mom sees it too, pours coffee. 'It's done, Adam, let it go. A rain, a breeze, and a warm spell ...' Gail laughs and shines. 'A little perfect weather and we're back in business.' She stands up and walks over to the window. 'Yup, looks like a nice one...' in a wrong voice. It's not funny, but mom laughs. 'You've got the right idea, but farmers only talk about what can go wrong with the weather.' Adam makes a funny noise, and then he laughs too, a little. 'Talking about anything good is just asking for bad luck.'

Gail turns around and goes back to the window and talks to outside. 'I didn't mean it...just joking...you're an ugly, pathetic excuse for a day...I just didn't want to hurt your feelings...' and now he laughs bigger. 'Too late, we're already jinxed...sit down and have breakfast while it gets ready to pour.'

Then he gets small and doesn't talk. Mom drinks coffee. 'What's everybody doing today?' She gets up, and looks back at him. He thinks. 'Brooding.' Nods. ' I think I'll brood.' I think about what to do too. 'Let's go to the orchard and see how they're getting better from the medicine.'

He makes the funny not funny noise again, the sound of Sam sneezing. 'See our poison apples...who'll want the load?' It's quiet. 'Maybe we can sell the whole crop to Snow White Specialty Products.' Gail smiles. 'Healthy eating...plus it promotes long, deep sleep...' Only mom still has her right colour. 'It's done Adam, you had to, now let it go.' It's her right voice, but from before, and it's everywhere in the kitchen.

Her right voice. *Just you and me,* everywhere and I know my part *and baby makes three* and I'm looking at her waiting for her to start the sing together part *my blue...* but she's looking at me, they all three are and I get shy and laugh and Gail talks. 'Well, I'm off to the garden. We've got a boatload of zucchini and weeds.'

They both go out to their house and I look at mom and remember, and don't know. 'Why don't you sing now?' She's shy. 'It's not easy to explain.' She stays shy. '...gets harder...when you're...older...to sing.' She looks thinking. 'It just goes away. I don't know why.'

I think too, and she puts the dishes in the sink. 'You dry, please?' Looks at the towel as she turns on the water. When it smokes I squeeze the bottle, just right, it bubbles up, smells lemon, and she looks at the towel again. I put down the bottle and pick up the towel. She puts a plate in the water and hums. '...just you and me...' and I remember and see a man in the driveway and Prince running past him. I hum one word, and there's a feet on the porch sound. Mom stops washing; hears it too.

A boot, a clunk, a boot, boot clumk. I know it's Roger. He was Mr. black Mitchell, but now he's grey and heavy and a cane. Mom goes out to the mudroom and opens the door. 'Roger, come in. We haven't seen you in ages.'

His voice is big when it's right. 'Morning Alma. Why don't we sit on the porch for a minute? Nice morning. Waiting a while for it, eh?' Her voice changes to square. 'Why of course. If you'd like.' She goes out.

I hear their porch walks and the chairs scrape as they sit, and then his big voice from inside. 'Not much of a summer…till today anyway.' I can't hear hers.

Then he changes his voice and I can't hear, so I stop drying and sit down at the table. It's still shady in the morning. I hear them move the chairs again, and walk on the porch and I can hear her when they go past the window. '…No, that's ok. It won't be upsetting. Come on in …coffee?'

His voice is right again when they come inside. 'Morning, David, … you lads working to coax some fruit onto those trees ?…spite of all the wet?' He sits by putting his hands on the back edge of one chair and sitting down slowly onto the one next to it. I watch. He puts his cane hook over the back of the chair and mom waves her hand and puts out the mugs. 'David will you get the sugar bowl please?'

They have coffee. She's flat and solid when she talks to Roger. '…He's taken off for days before. What made them think this time is different? Weeks even, I've heard.'

He drinks. Looks at me and then at her. 'They didn't say exactly.' He sits. Looks. 'Just somehow the place felt funny. Deserted. They launched off there last week and he wasn't around then, either.' He spoons sugar and stirs.

Mom doesn't drink hers. 'Did they go inside?'

Mr. Mitchell stirs and drinks, and some gets on his beard. 'They didn't say they did; …but they mentioned the door was open, I think.'

We're all quiet; mom looks at the table. 'Well, thank you for telling me. I think I'll ask Adam and Gail what they think before we do anything.'

He finishes drinking his mug. 'You do that. ' He sits still. 'Good coffee, Alma, thank you.' Mom has the pot. 'Have some more? Shouldn't let it go to waste.' He shakes his head. 'Too much rots my gizzard now. Everything I like seems to do.' He sits still. 'Now I've got my chores to do or the place will run down on me. He looks at his cane and stays sitting. I stand up. 'I have to do my chores too.' Mom stays sitting until he reaches out both hands to the back of the chair with his cane on it, turns it around to be close to him, and holds on to that when he stands up and takes his cane. His breathing makes a squeezy noise. 'I see where Adam sprayed yesterday. No getting around it this year?'

Mom stands quiet. 'Yes. I mean no. There isn't.' He goes out with mom, and they say good-by on the porch and she comes back and we start back to our chores again.

We take all the things off the kitchen table, and put them on the counter. I wipe them and mom polishes wax on the wavy table wood. I put the placemats and all the things back on their places. We sit and rest.

I hear feet in the mudroom, and Gail comes in for lunch with a box of zucchini and onions and dirty hands. 'Rain or shine, here they come.' Mom takes the box and we look. 'They're small. Lots more?' Gail nods. 'Lots and lots.' Adam comes in too, with no colour, and goes on through to wash his hands. Mom is a nice pale blue looking at pink and green vegetables. I'm happy. She hands me the box. 'Put this outside for now, please, David.' She sets the table.

It's quiet while we eat. When we're almost done, Gail says zucchini love this weather. 'We'll have so many... shall we try making relish with them?' Mom looks surprised. 'We won't have enough cucumbers?' Relish comes from cucumbers? Adam gets light and red and laughs. 'Trouble ahead. I've brought a dangerous radical into the house. Next thing she'll have you making yellow salsa from the green tomatoes.'

Mom's voice laughs. 'Anybody who can find a use for zucchini should win a prize. What do you put in it?'

'Nothing special... it's just salsa... poppy seeds, garlic, ... whatever's on hand.' There's lots of colour and the sounds are right, rolling along, but different than yesterday. I can make the sound bounce too. 'Mr Mitchell came over to visit this morning.'

Adam looks at me, then over at mom. 'How's the dodger?' His voice is different now... sharper.

Hers too, and she waits before she doesn't answer. 'Do you think you go and pick up the things for the relish? This afternoon, maybe?... and if you have time, look in at Fred's?'

Adam and Gail sit still. His voice is even. 'Why go by Fred's?'

I know the answer. 'He left the door open.'

Adam looks, at me and at mom. No colour or shape, and mom stands up and starts to clear the table. It's very still, and Gail looks at me. 'Let's do hornworm patrol this afternoon, David. They're attacking the tomatoes.' Her voice is soft, and I look at her yellow hair when she talks. 'It would be a big help.' I'm very good at catching hornworms, and her hair is light brown and yellow and a little is grey by her ears with silver circles and I remember it was more yellow the time they moved into the house behind our house. Mom washes dishes. 'I'll dry today, David. You help Gail.'

I go up to put on my work clothes; *remember* his hair was bright red Mr black Mitchell said *call the fire department here comes a flaming head* and I cried and dad laughed '...it's ok Davey, we're having a joke...' and when I come back the car is gone and we work in the garden.

We don't watch tv as much in summer, but tonight we do. Adam sets up the folding table in front of the set, and mom brings in applesauce. Gail carries the corn and I have the plates and butter on a tray. Adam arranges chairs, and we're ready. He gives me the remote, and I click. 6:01 pm. In winter that's Andy Griffith on 654, so I press that. Today it's the one when Otis loses his hat. We watch and eat corn on the cob, and the sounds of dinner and tv are grey and even. Mom and Adam go back out to the kitchen and I hear them. Their quiet voices mix in up and down with Andy and Barney. Gail goes out too and I hear them whisper when Otis comes in to the office and it sounds wrong so I turn up the sound. He reaches for the door handle and falls down when Aunt Bea opens the door at the same time and Andy says they have to carry him. Then a commercial, and the music sounds pointy and rough and I click the sound off and hear them talking in the kitchen. Adam's voice low. '...a coon in the house...boat gone...always feels odd, but this is different...deserted...' His voice quiet, then mom's sharp. '...what to do...' Gail's, soft. '...OPP?' ...Adam's quiet '...wouldn't know what to tell...' Barney is at his desk now and Otis is ready to go out and I know that Barney is telling Otis to let himself out and Otis is saying he doesn't have the key this time but I don't turn the sound back on and hear mom's whispery voice '...upset him...' and Barney and Gail's '...sure that sometimes you're not being too careful?'

A cupboard door opens, closes, Gail's voice '... have to know at some...'

Then no sound in the kitchen and Andy comes in. I turn him on and he talks to Barney. I know what he says but his tv voice is too shiny when they look for the key and I click off the sound. My leg jiggles and I don't want to watch. I get up and take the dishes out to the kitchen. There's no colour and mom is looking in the fridge and Adam is gone and Gail looks at me and mom's back and the empty table and at me and shines a little. 'Thank you, David.' She takes the plates to the sink, and when I don't go back to the den, '...sit with us for a minute?'

I do; we're quiet together sitting.

The next day is very warm, and outside is dark blue and shiny when I come down. Gail comes in and mom gives her coffee. 'Thanks Alma... Adam went up to look at the trees...'

I get cereal and mom gives me a spoon. 'He won't see anything yet?...'

Gail is yellow in summer. 'I know.' Drinks coffee. 'He knows.' Stands up and looks out. '...calling for sunny, and twenty five...' I sit down and she does too. 'He knows he'll be looking at nothing but that's better than not looking at something. Or something like that...' Mom laughs, small but right, looks around at the window. We hear Adam's feet and he comes in. 'morning.' We all look at him. 'Too soon to tell...'

He gets coffee, drinks, sits. It's quiet, and he stands. Looks out and says the words mom used to sing, but in a wrong voice. '...nothing but blue skies...' I hear morning doves low in the quiet, and he fixes his voice. '... maybe we'll get lucky...' *nothing but blue skies...* He sits. *never saw the sun, shin' so bright...*' 'Did you call Dorrie?'

'I will after breakfast.' She looks at me. 'Then we can set ourselves up to make relish. And you?... have you made any calls?'

He gets cereal and Gail gives him a spoon from the jug. He chews cereal and it's quiet and he looks at me and the sound of birds I don't know. He's red but not bright. Sees me looking and talks. 'I went to Uncle Fred's yesterday, but he wasn't home. Roger says he hasn't been around and we're worried that something might have happened to him.'

He doesn't call him Mr. Mitchell. 'What something?' He finishes his cereal and stands up. I look and can't tell if the colours are right, his voice is different but not wrong and I'm mixed up. 'What something happened?'

He sits back down. 'We don't know.' He looks at mom and his voice is right but funny. 'When I went by there yesterday, I just got a feeling from how things looked, and it made me worried.' He's my red brother sitting still in the brown chair at our table. ' ...ask the police to see if they can help.' He keeps sitting still, looking at me and mom does too. 'He has gone away... on little trips before, and maybe that's what this is.'

I'm calm and we can start our work now and we'll learn where he is. 'What does he do when he trips?' Adam smiles small and even and answers while I pick up the dishes and blue mugs and mom calls Aunt Dorrie and I learn that uncle Fred never had a colour even though he was black sometimes and mom stops talking and hangs up. 'Will you get the black stove pot and the jars David?' Gail turns on the radio for us and goes out to do her chores and mom turns back around to me. 'I mean please and thank you...'

Adam says the OPP say they can't do anything but '...keep an eye out...' for uncle Fred. It's hot and we have potato salad for dinner on the porch. We finish and sit and Prince barks. Mom isn't blue and she asks me to help take the plates inside, but keeps sitting still and Adam gets ready to talk. He has a card in his pocket in his shirt. 'Constable Perrault... one of the new ones... asked if Fred has ever gone away like this before?' He laughs. She asked me to check in on the house every so often and let them know.'

Gail laughs too and I look. 'What's funny?' His voice changes, and he's still talking to her. '...And bring them a tray of double doubles when you come by to report on their investigation.' Gail laughs, but I don't understand. 'What's funny?' Mom is shy and I put the plates on the tray, smell cut hay as I go inside, hear them talking. 'Maybe we could ask Roger who he's been paling around with this summer?'

The kitchen is beautiful and soft with nobody there and I can see the white pony through the window on the dark side. ' ...too old to go out on these little toots anymore... David, are you in there?' I touch the top part of the window knock, knock, and wave at him outside. We have spiders in the kitchen, but not many. I go outside and we sit and look together. Mosquito bugs and big clouds in the north and the sun makes them pink and grey and a four wheeler rides/ a bat!. The clouds move along and the sun makes the mullen along the fence be tall dark lines sticking up in a row and we sit.

'Maybe rain...?' ...he keeps sitting. 'Just one good one...' Mom sits too; her eyes are closed and Gail stands up '... check the weather...'

Adam points to mom and puts both hands with his palms together on one side of his face, and Gail moves her chair and it squeaks on the floor and mom shakes her head when Gail walks. Mom brushes her hair back off her forehead and stands up. 'I'm not tired', and Adam holds out his hand to mom and he talks while she holds it to stand. 'You go on up... David and I can do the cleaning . Maybe break the rules and watch tv for a minute later.' He looks at me. '...even though it's summer? Just this once?'

Mom goes out, and he turns on the water to let it run hot and I smell worms and make a face and he smiles. 'One week without rain and the well's down already.' He squirts in foamy soap. 'Maybe check the cistern while we think of it, and I'll be ready for you to dry.'

I get the flashlight and open the basement door, smell wet just-plowed dirt and stones, step down two and shine it on the water. One half, I know. I come back to the dishes. 'One half.' He cleans the grey counter around the sink and the silver faucet. *'One half...?'* He makes a face I don't know the name. 'One half full or one half empty?'

His *when is a door not a door?* voice is the name. I think, stop drying, listen, and learn the answer: 'Both of them,' and go back to drying. He laughs, just right, round and soft and red, looks at the clock. 'Almost 9:30... what'll it be?' I sing, in a maybe other people are sleeping voice. '... Just sit right down and you'll hear the tale...', and we go in to watch.

Saturday is grey and heavy, and all the colour is dull. I weed before the rain, and Gail picks hornworms and zucchini. The garden smells muddy and the wind makes the poplar leaves crinkle silver, and tomatoes too, she picks I go over and sniff, and hear the white pony sniff in the Smith's and a loud door noise, *slam* I remember, and pick up the weed basket for the compost. She sees me. 'Done already?'

I listen to the white pony and remember grey Sam and talk while I remember: 'We'll get all wet…' She looks up and listens. 'A good rain, you think? Wash off our apples?'

We go inside and mom is on the phone with Aunt Dorrie. '…no, nothing…'

I wash my hands and Adam comes in. I hear a car on the road sound clear in the quiet and he looks out as branches swing in the wind and the rain starts, and pats the window sideways, with his palm. We watch it and listen.

Mom hangs up the phone and stays sitting. 'Dee hasn't heard anything, and neither of the girls either.' She stays sitting. 'I don't know what to do.' The rain taps loud beside her voice, and makes it sound small. Adam looks back inside, at her, and talks louder than the rain. 'Nothing we can do.'

Mom taps the phone with her fingers. He talks. 'I guess we could have a look if it lets up…' She tap taps. '…give me a reason to check in with madam Perrault…'

After lunch Gail goes shopping in the car and the rain stops. There are shiny puddles in the driveway and the roofs drip. We all go out to the porch. Mom talks to Adam. 'That was what you wanted?' Adam is a little red, even though it's grey outside. 'The first part, at least. Now warm and sunny for…' He sees me watching and mom not listening. His voice is good. ' …take a ride in the truck, amigo? See what we can see down at Point Petre?' Mom sits. 'Wear your hats, lads. It could still drip a bit more.' We get in the truck, and Adam drives.

Little branches are down from the wind and leaves off the poplars even though it's still summer. It's grey and the clouds are in long fat lines, and the sun comes out between them and the wind blows branches in the road and the clouds roll back under the sun and we ride.

He turns into the stones on Uncle Fred's driveway and a big branch is in the way. 'Can you get that yourself?' I get out and lift up one end and turn it away from the driveway. It rains a little more and my hat gets wet and it stops.

We stop driving and look at the house. There's a stick leaning against the door, like our driveshed, and branches broken off and stuck in bushes, and thistles and weeds lie down flat in the yard. It's still grey but they're all shiny and I see the blue water blowing through the willows and some of them are broken and sideways too. I keep looking and Adam has no colour. 'Not much to see, eh?'

We get out and he goes behind the house and I hear gulls by the loud water and fish smells. I don't like it and I walk back up the driveway where we came. Stand; listen to the poplars. Adam comes out around the other side of the house. Still with no colour. I look through the weeds down flat from the rain and on to wet shiny dark trees and thorn bushes. See, shout. 'Adam, ... something red ...'

He walks over to me and we look. He folds his arms and looks but doesn't go there. I know *do what Adam does*, and fold my arms to look too.

'Can't picture Fred ever driving a Sienna, eh bub?' Sun shines and I look up. '... rainbow!' He looks. 'Wow ... a double ...' He looks back down at the red car. '... Go call this in, eh? They may want to come down.'

We walk back to the house. He takes the stick away from the door and we go in. Bathroom smell. The floor creaks and we walk through the hall. Dust, my nose wrinkles and we go in the kitchen. The phone is on the wall. He picks up the handle and listens. 'OK ... still works.' He calls and I listen. '... car in the woods ... no, only because the wind flattened so much brush ...' He talks louder. '... not till Monday? It might be important now ...', then softer 'ok ... so you'll call?' Then very quiet. '... yeah.'

Monday is light and the colours are good when I look out the window in my room but nobody has any colour when we have breakfast. We're quiet at lunch too, and when I take the plates away the phone rings and Adam talks. 'Yes, speaking.' Listens, thanks, listens. '... reported stolen? When?' Listens and the kettle whistles; and a crow. 'No, not as far as I know ...' He holds the phone and talks to mom. 'Did Fred ever talk about a Sandy Dainard?, ... do you remember?'

She shakes her head and he talks to the phone. 'No, although we certainly didn't know everybody. He didn't make many new friends as far as we know of.' He listens. 'Yes, we are concerned. Is there anything you can suggest? ... or tell us? ...' He listens again, and we sit still.

He hangs up and sits back down. 'The red Sienna was reported stolen two weeks ago. Registered to a Sandy Dainard. In Kaladar.' He stops, looks away, starts again. 'They didn't say if that's a man or a woman ...' He's quiet, looks at mom and there's no colour in the warm summer room.

'She said that there isn't anything they can actually do. She was polite and apologetic, but she said that if he is safe and healthy, he will most likely come back voluntarily ....' No colour, no sound and mom puts her hands one on each side under her chin and looks out the window.

It's warm and bright the next day, and the days after too. We walk up to the orchard and the apples turn redgold and Gail brings in orange tomatoes for mom. Their colours flash on and off and the tomato smell jumps and sparkles. Aunt Dorrie and Amanda come to visit and I watch tv even though it's summer. Their voices waver up and down, and sometimes all three go together with perfume and I'm sad. I hear their car go down the driveway and I go back and mom is sitting at the table looking at the blue and white teacups and the ashtray smells burned.

Then it gets too hot even though it's the end of summer and Gail and Adam wear shorts and I weed and wash the car. It's still morning and I pick beans and tomatoes for mom and wash them off outside with the hose and she puts them into their right baskets. Mr Vincent and his nephew come in with their green harvester and baler and mow Smith's field and then ours. They leave the machines in the field and drive away in their white trucks and come back and keep mowing after lunch. It's very hot and I watch the hawks float and dive in the fields when Mr Vincent drives. The baler stops and they both come to talk to Adam. Mr Vincent makes a spinning shape with his hands, and Adam gets the tools and we all ride back out to the field where the baler is. We stand together at the back and lift the cover and look inside. Adam unbolts the reel and pulls away the twine from the teeth. It's in pieces, and he puts it back together. I tie the pieces of green binder into a ball in my hands. Mr Vincent gets back in to drive the baler and his nephew looks at red Adam's shorts. ' ...ready to pack those up for the year now...?' He laughs and Adam smiles. 'Why's that, Charlie?' Mr Vincent waves as he starts to drive and his nephew gets in their truck to ride us back. 'You haven't heard? Calling for cold, Adam. Tonight. He looks, little smiles. 'Thought you fruit guys stayed all over that weather channel news. Yeah... summer ends on the last day of summer this year, with a kick in the pants.' Adam loses his colour. 'Frost?' We get in the truck and he drives . 'Yes sir and madam, and the real deal if they're right.' We ride and it's quiet and bumpy.

Adam puts the tools away. 'Let's walk up and have a look.' Up the lane and the poplars are dropping leaves and the maples are green and the orchard is pink and green and gold and the sky is smooth blue and Adam is right red. *Do they see me blue?* It makes me chilly and he picks an apple and takes a bite and gives it to me. 'What do you think?' I chew sweet.

We sit at the table. Listen to the weather '...unseasonably cold the rest of the week...' and Adam shakes his head. 'Just crazy...' Mom is soft. 'You've had a real run of good luck this month.' Gail is dull. '...just what the global warming model says...' Adam stands up and she keeps talking. '...wacky and extreme and...'

Mom folds her hands on the table and looks tired. '...sounds like business as usual...' Adam nods. '...well, they're about ready...what do you think, David?' I say what I think. '...sweet, crunchy, pink...' and they laugh, even mom.

He stands up. 'I guess I'll have to finish getting the loader put back together...get the boxes up there and hit it Friday?' Gail shrugs her shoulders. 'I'm in for all of it, I guess.' She goes to watch the same weather on tv. They both have bright colour and I'm ready to *count me in* too.

Next morning is sharp and blue and Adam is already outside when I come downstairs. He's got his check shirt and red winter hat. I go out through the mudroom. Cold hands morning and I see him bringing the boxes out of the driveshed where pink Sam lived and putting them in front piled up and little white frost tips on the grass up the lane and the fields where the no leaves poplars make purple line shadows on the boxes.

I go back in and have cereal and Gail comes in. She has a grey sweatshirt, eats cereal too. 'Better get your sweatshirt, David. It'll be chilly...' She gives mom her bowl while mom talks to me. 'It's in the front downstairs closet, David.'

We go out past the big black shadow of the house into the crunchy lane together carrying the baskets. Crows land in the field and fly up again. Adam pulls the forks out from under the second box and we go up that row under the geese in a point, it smells clean and we look. 'Some of those are too small...those too...take off that whole side when we're done...' I look at her, the small yellow apples with brown spots crow sounds shining in the fall. '...let's keep them separated out.' Adam comes back. '...get the next two later.'

I like picking. I do the good ones first... more geese in a line and the shadows are small following when I walk back to tip my basket gently in the box and she walks with her basket sitting on her head held up by one arm and looking up at bright red Adam in the next row looking back laughing.

We fill two boxes and the colours are bright at suppertime. ' ...not a great crop, but maybe ok...' They laugh. Adam's low voice. '...maybe ok.'

The next day is even brighter. I'm very happy. We walk up the lane together in our sweatshirts and Adam points down. 'Deer last night?' They have big grey socks today. Duck sound little birds chase a hawk behind geese high and I turn around to look in the sun and walk around myself to backwards under the geese. I keep turning where the grass shines and they're holding hands walking ahead of me I'm a goose too keep turning around to walk backwards again then around and flap my arms keep turning to finish *blue goose* walking to the orchard frontwards to do the little ones today with spots where he puts the pink tape pieces on the limbs to cut off for green firewood when we're done.

Adam has one box on the side for the seconds and we fill it and go back for lunch. Mom has the radio on while she cooks and they take off their sweatshirts and we listen, have lunch. It's soft and smooth when they talk and the phone rings sharp. Gail reaches out. 'Hello.' She loses her colour and passes it to Adam. He talks, the radio talks, they all sit very still. Geese lines in the blue window and blue plates on the brown wood table. He listens, grey spoons and white napkins -they all sit very still no colour. '...Bon Echo!?' Sharp and wrong and he keeps listening. '...yes, ...no... can I do it by calling them?'...listens... 'Thank you, corporal, I appreciate that...' He sits and the phone sits in his hand.

The radio says '...Friday sunny and cool, with a high...' and no sound, no colour, and mom is very small. 'I guess I knew already...'
He's big, and looks down at his plate and at Gail, at mom. '...they did say that it was likely...' Mom stands up and picks up her plate. She reaches for mine, stops moving. The light is on even though it's day and the window is bright. She puts the plates down again. Gail's chair scrapes, the radio, a truck on the street, and mom sits. Puts forks and knives on the top plate, keeps sitting with her fingers on the round sides of the plates. 'I mean I knew it would be something like...' She stops. I'm confused. Adam breathes in holds the phone to talk but Mom talks before he starts. ' ... what did they?...' I jiggle. Mom puts her hand on mine tapping. 'David.' I'm still now and she talks. 'Adam...what did they say?'

He puts his hands in his lap takes another breath in the quiet and talks smooth but not his voice. ' ...inform you that a body matching the description of Fredrick Bongard was recovered from a marshy area in Bon Echo Provincial Park yesterday by police responding to a call from a hiker. It was covered over and partly decomposed.'
His voice changes to his, kind and flat. 'She was polite and sympathetic. They need permission to get his medical and dental records to confirm the identification.' Mom shakes her head, first sideways and then up and down. 'If they need dental records, he'll pass on forever unknown.' I know she's sad, and Gail stands up and turns the radio off and takes the phone out from Adam's hand and hangs it up. 'I don't know if he even went to the doctor...do you? I remember Donny said you'd never get that man to a doctor. Maybe a vet...' She looks at me, at Adam and Gail, and back at me.

'You know what we're talking about, don't you?' I think. The salt shaker is glass, a silver top with 5 holes and rice and salt. She keeps looking. No rice in the pepper. Looks. 'Yes or no, David?' The soup spoons are silver and one is different. I'm thinking as hard as I ... 'David yes or no?' I look at her. 'Both of them.' She looks back and talks.

Sun in the window and talk. Adam phones a doctor's office. '... retired?...right...I guess...do you have a home phone?...' He laughs. 'Thanks, but I won't call Florida information...yes, thank you.' Gail clears the plates. '...did he have an OHIP number?' Mom stands up and turns on the water. 'I think maybe; yes...' Adam stands still and I get the dishtowel. 'He had some papers and tools and fishing gear in the front room...registrations and stuff...but I never saw anything like an OHIP card.' I dry. I work carefully. They sound almost right but my hands shake a little, and I dry very carefully. Mom puts the spoons in the basket, looks at me, and looks down at the sink as she empties the dishwater, and talks to Adam. 'Will you go down and see?' She looks at me, and her eyes are like when she's reading. '...when you're done.'

He takes his sweatshirt off, and folds it. It's quiet and I'm ready to go back picking. His hair was I remember like pumpkins, or when tomatoes were almost ready. The names hum. Now it's darker and white fizz by his ears. Dark, rumpled, red brown. I can hardly hear them. 'Maybe I'll go now. I'll just be thinking about it anyway.' Gail stands up. 'We can keep working...it's going fine.' He stands but doesn't go. 'Maybe David and I can run down together...there's a lot of junk to go through...' Mom sits back down and holds up her chin with her hands. I can't see what she's looking at. 'David, would you give me the phone before you go. I'll call Dorrie. Please.'

We take the truck, and I open the window. It's loud with the wind. The maples on the road are yellow when the ones on the lane are still green and the sun runs along on the hood, around the cab and in the window when we turn down the road to Point Petre. Adam has no colour and he turns down the flap to keep the sun out. He's shy. The visor. 'David, Uncle Fred died.'

His voice is soft and wrinkled and flaps in the wind, but it sounds right, and *uncle Fred died, but we're going to his grey house near the water. At Christmas Aunt Dorrie and Amanda and Steph and then the boys came to visit for dinner but not uncle Fred except once.* My hands shake and I wiggle my knees. *Uncle Fred died and Sam died and we buried him to rest and before that one day dad went out and mom said he passed and couldn't come home.* I jiggle fast look at Adam. 'Why?' We went past the big house with the long white fence and the Jersey herd on my side are standing in the same direction. Adam drives. 'We don't know, exactly.' He looks ahead. 'That's why we have to get some papers and cards to give the doctor.'

He slows down, flips up the …visor, and turns off onto uncle Fred's driveroad. He drives along slowly on the stones and looks at the goldenrod, purple asters and a round black place on the side. 'Somebody's had a fire here…' and we drive into the yard.

He gets out and walks on the porch and takes away the piece of wood closing the door. He turns the doorknob with this hand, but it doesn't open. He spreads his legs out, makes a noise, and pulls it open *squeaky* starts to go in and stops. Looks back at me sitting in the truck. 'It's ok, bug.' I tap. He looks. *We all live in a yellow submarine* walks back to the truck, '…really, it's ok.' His voice is right and I get out *submarine* and we go in together. The room we go in is almost empty. There's an alternator on a table, an empty cup…Adam walks ahead *and a friend, is all a board,* turns around and looks at me. 'It's ok.' The air is sad and dusty and I follow Adam. We go in another room; it's almost full up. He looks. '… somewhere in here,…if at all…' Goes to a desk and looks in the drawers, and opens a dresser with magazines and papers but not clothes. 'I don't know, bud, anything could be anywhere here…'

The window shade is down and it's almost dark. I tap tap the table. He sees. '…not exactly a cheerful spot, is it?' I nod and tap. '…but this is something we should do for mom, and her brother.' I'm very still. 'Brother?!' 'Um hmm, like you and me…well, except she's his sister, like Steph and Amanda…' I think hard. *Sister?*

He picks up a box of papers and goes out and puts it on the table by the alternator. 'I think we should look around, together.'

Upstairs smells very bad *died.* Flies in the windows on the floor on the bed and the clothes on the floor and the other room too. They died *dead.* We go back down the creak in the quiet house stairs. His tackle box is on the table, I hear water now and the fridge is loud and 'Adam my nose hurts'. He laughs, nods. 'I said we'd look around, but you have to draw the line someplace.' We go back into the desk room and Adam gets papers into another box and looks in drawers and takes one drawer out and puts more things into that and looks around. He doesn't talk and I watch him move and *uncle Fred is dead as a fly, and Sam,…big and soft, grey and ate grass* he goes out, sniffs. 'OK, …we can look this stuff over back home.'

We each take a box and a drawer and go out to the sun coming in between the trees and the lake wave sounds *dead* and put boxes behind the seat and he comes back to close the door. 'Let's go, eh? Had enough of this place for the short term?' I put the drawer in my lap, and the smell is in the truck now. 'Funny thing, hombre... I've never been inside there before except once. When you found the van...?' Adam drives. '...didn't really know him, did we? Do you remember anything about him?' Mom talked once in her talking to Aunt Dorrie voice. '...doesn't laugh he crackles like a crow...' *Dad died he was tall, his hands I remember were red, Sam died, big his eyes were and black and we dug him in the pink rock ground* and Adam turns out onto the road. Knock my foot. Knock something waiting for me to learn it that way shifts up and drives *the other night dear* I'm chilly won't go away try harder *when I awoke dear*, no *I was mistaken* have to look it's very chilly how do I know it's waiting ask what I have to learn. 'Will you die?' The sun is in the side window now and he drives slow it's in my eyes between the trees but I don't put the visor... over, and I don't think of something else, I'm learning, 'Yes,...' his quiet voice '...someday.' The one by one trees go by, slowly as he drives, and I look at him and he looks away from driving and I learn and he talks. 'Not soon, I hope, but someday we all will die.' I'm cold, tap my fingers *no I but I look.* Don't think something else and it comes in the truck and sits as he turns onto our street and the sun runs through the windshield and makes everything bright and gold and his voice was right and *I'll die too* lands *hung my head* in my stomach *and cried...* sits lumpy, *me, me too* heavy as he goes in the driveway.

The next day is cloudy and quiet and we picked two more rows into the boxes. A rock, it feels like but bigger. It went away when I was outside in the orchard, and then came back when we went in the house for lunch and went again away up the lane. When we finished picking and walked back there was a car I didn't know in the driveway. Adam and Gail went in the mudroom with me and then on their house. 'We'll be right back.'

I go inside. Aunt Dorrie was there with Amanda and a smooth little red girl with black hair I didn't know sitting at the table drinking tea. They all smiled and looked at me. 'Hello David, hello...' Their voices and smells are crooked and I'm shy. Mom looks at me. 'You must be tired David... did you three work hard today?' They all three looked at me being shy and I nodded. 'Why don't you go and wash up then, and we can visit later.' The red girl had blue eyes like dad's and I wanted to look at the colour. I washed up and put the dirty clothes in the laundry and when I came back downstairs they were gone. Mom was finishing the dishes and I reached for the blue towel, but she shook her head. 'Let's sit down and talk for a minute and then you can watch tv.' She sat down at the table and waited for me and we were quiet. We looked out the window but no geese and it stayed quiet. No colour. 'David?' I wish she would sing. 'Adam told you that uncle Fred might have died?' I sit still. 'The doctor looked at the papers you and Adam got, and they confirmed that it was him...that he died.' I sit still. She looks. 'Do you remember when dad died?' I nod. She talks. 'What did we say then? Do you remember?' I try to remember and I remember because Adam said yesterday. '...he had to go away and not come back..' I remember more. '...and you cried when I looked at the lazyboy.'

She sits up straight in her chair. 'You're much older now David. When somebody dies they aren't in a body anymore. Fredrick isn't, is what happened. I think you're old..., that you can come with all of our family to his funeral. When somebody dies they leave their body, and nobody knows where the person goes after that. They put the body in the ground, like we did for Sam, and the friends and family are there. They remember... it's sad...we behave in a certain way...like a doctor visit, to show that we don't want to upset other people ...' I hear her voice waver and blue...sit still...try very hard...remember *when we go into town we're quiet, no colours, no running*...and she talks '...this is difficult, because people are sad about Uncle Fred. If you do feel upset, try to think about something else...and be still. Funerals are very quiet *in the ground* and I want you to try as hard as you can. Do you understand?' I look she's blue and not blue *blue skies, nothing*...'I know it's upsetting...' She's not blue and a different blue. '...but you understand what I'm asking now?'

'Yes.' I sit. She looks, doesn't move. *like a big rock* 'Yes, as hard as I can.' I look, wonder *they all know like a rock?*

The next morning I wake up and look out. The clouds run in long lines and the maples swing in the wind and yellow leaves blow off in a circle when I watch. Adam is on the phone when I come into the kitchen and Gail is drinking coffee and mom comes in. He hangs up the phone. 'They're coming down in an hour,...and I'll go back in with them after we decide.' *Decide?*

I don't hear the wind on this side of the house. Gail is standing up and taking mom's cup out. One row left and rain tomorrow. Adam looks at mom, and I get cereal, and he looks at Gail. Can you guys do the last row this morning while we talk? You'll have to take up another box? It's dark out the window in the morning but getting lighter when we pick apples and I wear my sweater. Gail drives the loader and I steady the box while she gets it on the forks and lifts it up off the ground. She puts in the clutch and waves to me with her hand moving toward her. I look and walk over to her. 'Ride on the back, or walk up...?' Geese fly over...way up but we hear them honking and the sun come between a cloud line. 'Neither one...' I shout over the engine and wave my arms. 'I'll fly,' and I fly in circles turning around up the lane and when I pass the barn I turn to be looking back and a black car comes in the driveway. '...come on big bird, let's get picking...' I stop flying and start jogging.

We finish picking and it warms up and we take off our sweaters. Her face is shiny. '...almost eight this year, ...think they'll be good?' She picks up one and throws it toward me in a funny way so it floats high up and come down where I put out my both hands to catch it. When I catch and look back at her she's got one too and holds it up in front of her face and looks at me. 'To the pickers.' She bites, I remember toast, and bite too. She's yellow. 'Tastes like a wet summer, eh? but not so bad either...' She chews. I take another bite and she throws hers off to where the crows fly circles in Burrit's. The white pony isn't in its house and she throws in the same funny way. I picture and laugh and remember and look over to the pink rock and think as hard as I can and throw mine too the right way and it flies, the crows fly away, and lands in the tall gold grass and when I turn she's getting the loader forks under the box and turning around slowly. When she's done turning she waves at me and points back to the house. I walk and the sun comes around and hits the little window at the back of the barn and it shines. I'm walking alone and the sad comes in a lump and the sun is bright *we all live* I miss the colours *in a yellow* I remember when she came to visit first and mom still sang and Gail sang wrong too sharp then low and Adam laughed and mom's face was funny too and how her yellow song was new and funny and I liked how it made her look yellow too. '...a yellow submarine...' she sang wrong, '...with our friends.' that made Adam laugh and '...are all a board...' and then mom too. I walk and remember. The black car is gone now and I have to try very hard. I go up to where she's parking the *friends aboard* loader *trying hard* and she turns it off and sees me and laughs. '...what are you humming there, Ringo?'

Mom and Adam are sitting and it's quiet. He looks. 'All done?' She looks. 'Done.' Mom looks, and Gail talks. 'Seven and a half.' He waits. 'Try them?' She nods, he asks. 'Watery...?' She nods. '...but not as bad as you thought.' It's very quiet. She looks at them both. 'So you have a plan?' He looks at her, and at mom. Back to her. 'Williamson's. Friday. Just us... and a few of his buddies...no out-of-towners to wait for...and no church. Just Ms Clarkson. And the rest of the deal. Dorrie is having people over after. You guys must be starved?' Mom stands up. 'Yes, we have a lot to get started on. Lunch and to work.'

The next day we go into town. Mom cooks for Aunt Dorrie and Gail cleans our house and their house. Adam calls to get the apples for pressing. '...Thanks, John...We did expect it...First of next week?...'

Mom needs potatoes. They're busy, and I go in and turn on the tv and sit in the lazyboy but they don't have any right programs and Adam comes in. 'It's too early, David, unless you want to learn pilates.' I don't know pilates. I click the tv to mute. 'No...I'm too full to learn. I'm already trying as hard as I can.'

He laughs a red flash, and the sad thing *when the red, red* picks up the clicker and shuts the tv. 'We're full up, amigo, it's true, and we've got to make room for more.' He stands still. 'Why don't you come into town with me? Mom needs us to shop, and there are special clothes we have to wear tomorrow.' I try hard. 'OK?' Mine is smaller. 'ok', *robin comes* and we go.

I lie in bed; hear the rain. Mom walks down the hall and down the stairs. Small feet. My stomach hurts *rain, rain, go away* it goes away and rain on the window. Mom calls from downstairs. 'Come on, David; time to get up.' It's dark in the morning. We're going to the funeral today and I have to turn on the light.

When I come down they're having breakfast with the lights on. Adam gets up and looks out. '...really coming down...' We sit and have breakfast. It's very quiet, and we sit.

Adam picks up the bowls and goes over to the sink. 'We should get moving...' He stands still. '...umbrellas...we'll need them.. Mom picks up the other dishes. 'You get changed. What about shoes? Did you get them yesterday? I know where the umbrella is, and they'll probably have them at Williamson's too.' It's raining and there's no colour. Adam looks back at mom '...no shoes. Shit. Sorry...'

She puts the dishes in a pile by the sink. I eat cereal very carefully and Adam stands still. 'You look like you want to say something.' Mom looks at the dishes and starts to wash and speaks very soft. 'I still have some of Donny's...in the closet.' There are five spoons but only four of us and mom dries them without waiting for me to finish my cereal. Adam waits. 'Time to move, David...do you have the clothes you bought yesterday?' They're on a steel hanger in a plastic wrapper in my room. I finish my cereal and keep sitting.

She stops drying spoons and looks. 'Remember what we said yesterday?' Yes, and *the sad* look outside *rain, rain* no geese in the rain yes, five spoons and my clothes in a bag and she stands holding '...please, then try...' the spoons. 'I know we can do this together if we try.' She's small and quiet; I get up and learn: this is my chore for today.

I come down with my creaky new clothes on and Adam is sitting in the kitchen with his different clothes too. Black pants and white shirt and the same shiny cloth in his hand that I have in mine. He looks at me holding it and I remember. Red and blue stripes, and it goes in a knot. He smiles, and I remember then *necktie...try very hard today* 'Let's do this together, bud. Or maybe it will take all four of us...' My new shirt is pointy and the buttons don't fit at the top. I sit down and he tries to fit my buttons and the pants are tight and it hurts. 'It hurts, a little...' He does them all up but the top one. 'Maybe open your belt a notch there, David. Looks like you've got yourself roped in pretty tight.' I do, and Gail comes in from their house with black pants too and a black jacket and a very white shirt and little white stones shining on her neck and her ears. 'Let's see you guys in ties.'

Adam turns, '...do what I do.' We turn our collars to pointing up and put the ties around them *necklace it is* and he reaches around behind mine and puts the end over the top and shows me. 'Watch, ...now slide that through the front...' I try very hard *necklace, and I'd like to touch the white stones there's a word too* I try not *white like her shirt but softer and harder* he reaches over and pulls the tie almost tight. '...slides up and down on the back piece...?' I nod and we both slide our ties. 'We'll button the top button and slide the knot up to the top when we get there...right?' Mom comes in with a dark blue dress and big shoes and a black umbrella and holding more black shoes by their looped together laces. Adam and I match them into pairs and tie them on. She looks at all of us and the kitchen and the window '...raincoats?' We go out. My shoes don't fit and I walk bumpy. *Try* I try as hard as I can.

We go in the car Gail bought. *Toyota*. Mom and I sit in back and Adam drives with the wipers. It's very hot and my shoes pinch and sharp at the back of my foot no colour and the orange leaves blow up and in circles around us and Adam drives. Mom smells wrong. I feel funny and I push the button to open my window. The wind coming in the opening makes a sharp noise and Mom looks over. '...too hot for you, David?' I nod. 'Just a little bit open, then.' I push it up a little more closed and smell the rain air. The wipers whishy, swipe, and we're quiet. I twist sideways and put my nose into the window opening and smell wet. 'David.' Adam stops where you see out to East Lake. Mom says 'David'. I untwist and look inside. 'We agreed we'd try...' I sit facing frontwards, and *Yes, I remember*. I put my shoes and my knees together into a straight line. I'm itchy and he drives on past the cemetery with the orange Kubota digging cold dirt in the sideways rain and windy leaves.

We go on Main Street where you wait for the right colour and Adam turns left and then into a driveway for a very big house. There are square rocks on both sides and little trees growing by them in the rain. It's very quiet. The little tree branches touch the Toyota and make a bad scrapy sound going by. Adam goes behind to a parking lot. My shirt itches. A man in a black raincoat stands under a purple roof, and he points at Adam in the rain. The roof is round and touches the house at one end. Adam drives up and the man opens mom's door and then where Gail is. Adam keeps the car still. '...you guys get out here...David and I can park.' He closes the windows from his seat and drives to park. My edgy shoe hurts one foot, and he turns off the engine.

'Ready?' Looks. 'Your absolute best shot?' I like his voice. 'Yes, I will.'

He opens the door and puts the umbrella out ahead of him. 'My clothes hurt.' He pushes it opened up and it clicks. '...mine too...here; ... hop under when you get out...'

He's outside holding it open and I will be quiet *my stomach hurts* the rain blows sideways and he holds the umbrella facing that way and we go in. A man holds the door open and closes it up after we go by. The room is grey and the ceiling is low. Mom and Gail are there and the rug is the same purple as the round roof outside with green curly lines. It sounds wrong and smells very bad *I want to go now*. Adam buttons his top button and slides up his tie to the top and then does mine and looks and I know *try very hard*.

Mom puts her arm in Gail's arm and they walk. She's smaller than Gail and her neck has a bend at the back and *it's very* hot and the sound is mushy and we walk down a hallway behind them and then low bumpy music in a room. Big with benches like a church, and a higher ceiling and white flowers on a shelf. Lights hang on wires and the same rug on all of the floor. I look at that and the windows and the lights again and the flowers hot and people sit on the benches. I look at them look away but I can't it's too shiny sitting there in front I stop walking and look, look, look it's on a metal dolly *very* tight I don't remember the benches are orange wood the name of the box between the white flowers their name either look, look at it the ceiling is pointed up to the roof with wood beams and long shadows Adam puts his hand on my back we walk to the people sit benches and I *Casket*, I remember and Aunt Dorrie and the black hair girl at our house here sit in one row and Stephanie and Amanda and two boys in the row behind clothes hurt Gail goes in a row to the black hair girl I remember *baby Miranda* visited with cousin Amanda 'your hair exactly Alma isn't it incredible?' Adam points I go in then Adam and mom and we sit down but mom looks squeezed in and Gail whispers to Adam and she gets up and goes to the orange row behind us and I move over next to baby Miranda and look at the **dark wood** ceiling beams and then over not a baby whispers 'Hi David' quiet perfect voice and I want to cry *I promised to try* sit up straight put my knees together straight line with my legs and my hands in my lap together look over 'hi' whisper the benches are very hard smells beets old flowers brake fluid and I look on the other side benches and some men sit together a little behind us ...I don't know them they don't have their ties on *raindrops* today on their hair heads shine in the lights and Mr Mitchell with them and at the back a bald man and a boy I don't know have big eyes and not the door we came in Adam whispers 'David' I turn back *scratchy and* hot around and a man comes out from a door by the casket *how do I know casket?* stands by the side of the casket 'Friends' he doesn't have his tie either *you are my* can't tell Adam his not red now hair has raindrops too because I'm trying '...we are come here...' the boys behind me have noisy clothes his voice very bad and raspy eight pairs of *beams* and eight big lights hang in the ceiling means sixteen *beams* in all dark brown clothes rub the box orange wood with metal keep my knees in the right line want to jiggle his collar has purple '...now join me...' boy kicks I turn around '...in song...' stops kicking looks Aunt Dorrie they sing hot bad purple rug dull sound brake fluid, very bad sixteen beams *itches* orange benches feel *try hard* kick I learn *in the box* white flowers orange *away from his body* uncle curly Fred *in the box* I know he's there *how?* They sing '...Jerusalem-em-em...' orange *blue skies* I can't '...sa-le-e-em...' my elbows tight to me try to move to two beats it hurts flowers rot stronger *nothing but* '...Jeru...' and a voice sings right note soft by me sweaty wiggle purple rug bad sound *tap* Adam rug reaches over touches tapping hand orange wood *smell* '...salem...' is perfect, floats high and right like a goose I look *baby black dress Miranda* sings *not a baby* black hair straight sings I shiver sharp collar *hurts* hot *in the* **casket** my damp feet, knees *keep the worms* she sings *remember* kick the **worms** I try, try '...sa-a lem...' hands and feet to singtime smell kick tap too Miranda and Adam each hold a hand she sings *try, promised can't hard as I* **can't** tears go **can't** little lovely voice flies *geese* honking **blue** *mom* cry on my cheeks red Adam squeezes my hand lifts we walk wet purple rug eyes look leave and the fat bald man and boy are Uncle Fester and Pugsley why here laugh don't laugh I know don't, cry and open to cool out door street air ...cars go...on the porch he holds my breathe cry breathe stop *remember* rain air *wake up*, Jerusalem-em-em *wake up* orange leaves *breathe* rain wind cars '...buddy it's ok, I know...' breathe slow '...you tried...' and he gives me a handkerchief. Trucks on the shiny street 'ok, you tried...' blue house across 'ok...' quiet singing inside *remember* 'Adam I remember ...what hasn't happened' wipe last tear 'a casket...inside...' Give the handkerchief *not really him* cool rain grey backhoe drives yellow past and Adam '...all sorry for him David...' hold out his hand for the handker/cry again and I tell '...not him..it...not him...cask...' sniff back in me...cry/chief '...you!' breathe rain 'alone' and he looks *not him but who in alone?* looks straight at I breathe in try hard remember *can't come* stand up like blue mom *back again* wants me to he looks straight *I remember* and the black truck shiny street stops...stops orange flying leaves sit blowing still in the air he's red looks I look alone in the casket try hard he 'it's ok' holds my hand '...bud, got it, I do now, we both do now...' breathe air and the truck drives away in rain blowing again now '...let's go visit aunt Dorrie...' down the front steps in the grey and around the house to the parking roof '...wait here a sec, ...keys.' He goes inside and comes back out. We walk together over to the blue Toyota in the flying orange wind. He clicks the doors, and we get in and drive.

No cars are at Aunt Dorrie's driveway. She's at the funeral. Adam parks on the street and we walk up the driveway with little spruce trees and bricks in the ground. He opens the white front door in the white bricks front wall. It smells cookies, clean the house, we go in, dark and stand in the hall. It's very soft. Adam looks, '...hold tight here while I...' moves his hand on the wall and it lights up. I laugh at his wet brown hair but he's red. 'Dorrie and mom and Steph and Amanda and everybody will be here soon,' and my hair is wet too. 'Let's dry off and we can wait downstairs.'

He goes and comes back with a towel. 'You know the drill—atten/tion!' I stand that way and he ruffles up my hair and the house is soft and quiet. I can't see out the windows. 'Does Aunt Dorrie live here by herself?'

He finishes drying '...mostly...' then dries his own '...sometimes Miranda or Lukey or Jake sleeps over...let's go sit down.'

The back room has four big windows with smaller windows in them. They look out on her yard leaves, white birches in a row, and other houses in the rain and cars parked. One has smoke out the chimney. There's a tv in the corner and we sit '...David...' on the chesterfield '...they've gone to bury Uncle Fred's body...in the ground.' Yes. He waits. 'Are you ok?'

Waits; ...yes 'Yes.' Try hard. 'It's what they do when he dies.'

Sit up straight. I can. We do. 'It's not really him. He left his body.' Breathe in, *Not really him*...breathe out. *I learned it.* 'Mom and Gail and Dorrie and your cousins, ...their kids...and you and me...we'll visit for a little while.' I sit up straight, breathe in. 'You can be with us or you can watch tv in here if you'd rather...' Try, *in the casket* very hard. A car goes out a driveway in the windows he looks too. 'I guess we can loosen up our ties now.' He slides mine down, and I unbutton the top *he crackled* and loosen up is slide down.

A door opens in the house. He looks at me, then it closes; I wonder *why?* ask 'Why?' He's red in the quiet room white chesterfield. He looks. 'Why do they all come here?' Quietly wait while he thinks, tells me. 'It's what we do...' We hear feet sounds '...when somebody's gone...' and doors, water runs, '...do you...?' talking in the house, something fell down sound '...what do you remember about...?'

More doors, and walking in the house and the door opens to our room '...him?' Aunt Dorrie looks in '...there you are...', looks at Adam. He looks back and she closes the door quietly.

'Would you rather stay in here?' I nod. He nods 'Where's the clicker?' Turns the tv on, gives me the clicker and stands up. 'I'll bring you a cookie.' Goes. I click 654. The screen says '**not subscribed—consult your provider**' and I keep clicking: weather news weather, dark and quiet with the sound off and the door closed and the tv light in the room flashes on the walls and afternoon is windy and dark in the big and little windows. Hit on the table top with my fingers. I sit still...knock knock my knee with the clicker. Tap then a tap, different, not me. Tap, tap, on the door. I sit still and Adam comes in. 'Cooky delivery.'

He stands in the light doorway and I get up and go over. 'No 654?...' He looks at the tv weather station. 'What's called for tomorrow?' There's no sound. I shrug, bite my lip, click the clicker. 'You ok in here? We're not staying that long.' I nod. 'What are you doing?' He's red and true and even. I'm blue, but not silly. Not straight and even like Adam. I shrug. 'Remembering now before, I think.' The tv changes to not flashing lights. He looks straight at me in the outside dark afternoon light '...us too, a bit.'

Looks and the tv room gets darker and I look past his shoulder and down the hall. He turns sideways...looks there too. The living room opens up pinky-white and glowing at the end of the quiet hallway, and we listen. People talking... *remembering.* Now I know.

The all at once talking is soft and furry. I know 'remember' already, and learn this *remembering* now too and we look at curly white Stephanie *is when they're all talking and it sounds like bubbles* pour *cousin* wine 'Why? ...do they?' He keeps on looking at the sound before he answers. 'We just do', and waits, looks, turns back facing me. '...or maybe for something to hold onto.'

I listen to the buzzy talking sound *hold on* go up and down, to rain hit the window and he looks. 'You know, you can too, amigo...remember, I mean. It's how you hold on. Just say what happened...'

He unties his neck-tie knot, the tv lights flash onto walls and chairs in the dark room, and winds it around itself into a loop on his fingers *remember* the lake water behind his house sounds like the living room talking sound up and falling and soft-moving like a cat we called...'I get mixed up.'

He was starting to leave but he stops. 'True.' Smiles red with his voice. 'It can be that.' He turns around. 'I'm going back in there. You watch the tube, and we'll get going soon.'

I pick up the clicker, and look at him standing still in the doorway not going where he said.

He's darker now; I'm blue. I know that? *It's not in the mirror, so how?* ...still in the door; standing. 'You know what, bud...?'

He takes his word air in. 'Don't worry about getting confused ...it's not actually the important part. Just think what happened, and say it, ...to yourself ...one thing at a time, as it comes to you.'

He's the right red,—'I'll try as hard as I can.'

'OK?'

He knows how to work when we work. One thing at a time, he says, and careful.

He goes out and I sit in the squeaky white chair *I can the tv try hard flashes yellow and pink and the fizzy remembering noise from the living room. Rain, soft chair squeaks. I remember a thing say it one at a time, carefully, is remembering...one at a time and I try...*quiet in the rain blowing grey afternoon and the houses outside light up...try says Adam remember tv flickers in the soft dark *remember curly black, crackled our house then when he smelled like medicine...dark then like now dark and dark in our front room people lights in the den and the kitchen buzzing confused he saw me in the dark room alone with the...'* ... *right idea there Davy...little too close in there for me and you?' He's black in the door against the kitchen light smells 'see more than you let on, eh? ...sometimes I catch you...Wish I'd come up with you plan too...oh well, too late now, for me or him or any of us...' Light between the black pieces of his standing up hair and his face in the shadow with the silver tooth shine dark '...looking at that hole in the ground, thinking who's next?' he crackles and '...only a casket between hungry worms and our rotten guts....' Crackles and the light goes out behind him sudden/ 'Fredrick!' Mom blocks it he's dark I'm learning 'How dare you?!' He crackles '...not stupid as you all think and no baby now neither. No reason to treat...' I learn now that's what the box is, medicine smell in the grey, mom's breath so deep I can hear it move in fast as he crackles '...sooner or later Alma, and only more trouble for you if later'/' Fredrick! ...' stops him fast and only quiet and his different now voice doesn't crackle,...'I know, Alma, ..just on my way away, right away'...another mom breath sharp in the dark and 'You're mean and careless and stupid ...and...drunk...' / '...said I'm on my...if you...' then his breath too '...sorry...about Donny, I mean.' He goes out and the light shines through...dad's in the..the...*

casket, in the ground mud ...I remember not come back...alone mud I don't remember now..crying too alone? She takes me upstairs she's shaking and breathing and crying too holds my hand very softly the other night dear I wait for my part think the sound of my sunshine my only singing upstairs...is how I learned to remember.

November is raining too and I look out the window at breakfast and try to remember what it looks like with colours. It's quiet and Adam drinks coffee and stands up '...think about wrapping it up for winter.' I think about winter and no words come. We go out to the driveshed and start to get ready for winter. Adam turns on the compressor and we blow air through the tools and the orange chain saw. He gets a file and shows me how to hold the saw with a clamp and run the file in the teeth to sharpen it. ...*showed me before*? He puts antifreeze in the loader while I sharpen, and another one in the gas line. 'Let's bring the tiller and stuff up by the door.' It's cold but we open the door and he turns the tiller on, and the trimmer too, and they run in the doorway. 'Want your headphones, bud?' I nod and put them on and watch the machines run quietly *blue skies, nothing but* the tiller stops and he quietly takes off the top and unscrews the sparkplug *blue skies* puts it in a little plastic bag and then on the hook over the tools *winter is coming* the trimmer stops too and I hang it on the back wall *geese are getting fat* and he waves '...off a sec, there's nothing running anymore.' I do. '...lawn tractor now, too.' We push it out without turning it on and have to pick it up and turn it ourselves to get around the loader and out to just outside. He turns that on too in the rain and it runs loud. I put my hands on my ears and he smiles. 'ok, let's go in for a minute while it runs.' We start to walk over to the house and he stops. '...or maybe get the blade out now while we're on this job anyway?'

We turn around and go back inside the driveshed. I get the headphones and put them back on and the lawn tractor stops. Adam stops and looks at everything, keeps looking. 'Ok, here's a plan.'

He pushes the lawn tractor further out into the rain and angles it off to the side. Gets in the yellow loader and backs it out, turns it around in the gravel in front of the doors and drives it in to where the blade sits on its dolly at the back of the driveshed and points at the chain on the side wall. *I remember* and take it over and he hooks it on the top of the blade *winter* and loops it around the arm of the bucket and '...steady her for me...I'll go slow...' sounds very quiet with headphones and I hold the blade with one hand and walk *winter* and he backs out very slowly and when we go outside the doors he waves me off and turns the loader around to make the hanging blade face out to the house. *Christmas is coming* and I take off my headphones. He gets down and comes over '...early to get it on, but the weather is so weird these days we could have a blizzard or go swimming tomorrow, eh?'

His voice is dull. '...bring the 4-wheel over...' I don't remember at first and then I learn again. He gives me pliers and gets the battery from its shelf. We go behind the driveshed to the old truck that takes the plowing blade. Rain; he knows how to work. Lifts the hood and leans in '...ok, pass the pliers?...please and thank you.' Works and I watch. He gets in and the can, turns it on, shouts '...ok, no jumping needed...hop in unless you want to walk in the rain.' I do and we drive to the loader *now I remember put the plowing blade on.* We look at the black rubber piece that goes on the bottom and he nods and I look and go just inside the open doors of the driveshed. 'ok...keep it clear while I lift this up.' He gets in the loader and starts it up. It's very loud. He lifts the plow blade up and then lets it down a little and stops and looks out the window at it and turns the loader off and gets out. He drives the truck up to the loader so the two front ends are facing each other and I know he'll bolt the plow onto its pipes on the front of the truck.

It rains harder and wind blows brown leaves. I'm quiet and he runs over to the doors to stand inside with me and claps his hands. When we breathe steam comes out and he claps more '...you cold?' He turns to see me nod. '...ok go on in...' Walks over to the workbench to get his gloves '...almost lunch anyway.' I'm sad, try to think *when the red red* bored comes *geese are getting* goes away *yellow sub* all confused *robin comes bobbin* sounds wrong and I go in the mudroom and take off my dirty boots and go inside.

At lunch it's quiet again and mom wears her sweater and pours soup. 'What have you fellows been up to out there? Sounds like lots...' Adam looks at me and back at her 'Lots is us...all buttoned up...the plow's ready for a blizzard...' Gail looks at me while he talks. She puts down her spoon, gently. 'Why the rush?...they're calling for sunny and twenty tomorrow...' She looks at him and smiles. 'We'll have plenty of time to hibernate soon enough.' I don't know hibernate; he shakes his head. 'Twenty in November? ...just keeps getting crazier...'

Tomorrow is warm like she said. We sit after breakfast and mom washes the dishes. Gail is yellow and talks to mom. 'Have you called the lawyer, Alma? Now that we have some time we can see about Fred's affairs...' I get up to dry. '...I assume he didn't have a will?' *Will?* Adam laughs '...or pay bills, file tax returns, or...' He stops. Mom looks at Adam at me at her. I start drying and try to remember *lawyer*. 'I don't even know where to start...do you Adam?'

He shakes his head. 'But we should talk about it...maybe with Dorrie too? If nothing else, there's the house. The waterfront property, I mean.'

He looks at Gail and I look out the window and she looks at me. 'I'd like to work outside today... David, will you help me clean up the garden?'

We wear gumboots. She shows me how to work. Pull up tomato stakes and put them off to the side. Roll up the plastic sheets between the rows and put them next to the stakes. It's blue and it gets warm and we take off our sweatshirts. *Blue skies*...Some tomatoes and cucumbers and potatoes are left on the ground. They're mushy and we put them in a bushel-basket, ... *nothing but*...We're quiet and dirty on the ground where we took out the garden and I pick up soft brown and drop it past my 'blue skies, ..from now on...' I'm happy. She's quiet. '...never seen...' Very quiet. '...shining so...' She looks at me.

'...bright...'

'That's lovely, David.' I stop. 'It's ok to sing while you work. Lots of people do. ...you have a lovely voice.' *Voice?* 'For singing...' She looks at the soft vegetables. 'We could start a compost for next year... let it rot over winter.' I know compost but I don't remember. I remember winter, hear geese and look up at one line flying high and then down up the hillside toward the orchard getting ready for winter. 'Shall we do the garlic next?' I look. 'You put it in over the winter, and it shoots up in spring.' Look up the hillside, keep looking. 'I'll show you...' She points her rake off to a row on that side. I keep looking where the pony was. 'Are you ok?' I nod, she looks, looks...'OK, I'll get the garlic...' I rake a row *winter* and she comes back with a little brown bag and we kneel in the dirt. '...make a little hole, like so..' A worm, put it aside and '...put it in, pat it back, easy peasy...' sounds good happy sad dirt worm geese...I look up, it's a big line, loud and '...we can turn the rest over for next year with the tiller.'

I look back down up the hill and back at the house. 'We can't with the tiller.' Look at her looking. Yellow. 'Adam ran the tiller down yesterday.' She smiles. '...quite a rush, wasn't he?...' I look at the row to plant before winter. '...suppose now I'll just have to run it back up.' Cold brown dirt is for planting. '...straight gas in the driveshed?' I nod. She walks. I rake the dirt in rows, rake while she looks and comes back. 'You're ok?' I rake, she holds out the little brown bag, looks right at me raking looking down. 'What is it, David?' I take the bag, look at Smith's where there are three bales piled up at the little house where the pony was '...nothing to do.'

She stops. 'We've got tons to do, no? Apples, garden, firewood...'

Yellow, and makes her voice sound like Adam. '...ready for winter...' and lifts up the brim of her hat to see me. Keeps looking. I smile. 'There's nothing to do in winter.' Look up the hillside. '...in the house...' and down at the row and back up the slope. 'I don't want winter.' ...comes out. She looks, looks down, looks up. 'You need a project.'

She's yellow, it's blue, brown warm fall and she stands still looking. 'Will you start planting while I gas up the tiller?' I kneel back down, put the little trowel into the dirt at the top of the row. See her walk, stop, turn, walk back to my side of the garden. 'What about piano lessons?' She watches me. I stop. Hold a garlic in two fingers over its trowel hole. 'I don't know how...' soft dirt smells and she looks '...what lessons are for, aren't they?' Touch the dirt, blue sky from down kneeling the field looks rough running sun and dark up the slope lines '...never use the dining room at all anymore...'

She's gold I look geese, hands on hips '...what do you think?' I'm shy kneeling over, feel myself smile looking away. Tap my fingers, hang my head down to look upside down past her where the running down orchard lines and Sam's pink hang under blue I'm silly '...David...?' raise my head to right side up don't move geese over honk *remember black and white feel when I* tap garlic dirt in my hands smells summer '...well?' runs out my fingers *cold, quiet dining room black and white falling in finger tap colours when ...know it will sound like is a different remember, ...touching cold keys* look Burrit's he's dead, *make their sound lines up and down cinnamon, dish soap,* looking... *red blue lemon falling one two three in a row,* Gail, *at me up, down, down, up again sit the round chair spins brown soft tap falling rise stop tap, down when I touch,* runs out *my running fingers* me and Gail *running smooth warm grey of my hands running backward Sam's hair falls runs touch on his neck he's still* me *sunshine* playing *me* touching *happy* the piano *when skies...*

...I had lunch waiting, but there was no sign of them. I went out, and stood on the porch to call. She was crossing the muddy driveway, walking over to the driveshed. 'Lunch. Gail—lunch. David...' I called, but maybe I don't have much voice left; she opened the shed door and went in, without turning back. I went inside, and took Adam's gumboots from the row,—they fit over my shoes. I tromped out, around back to the garden, and stopped in my tracks. He was kneeling there, in the garlic row, back to me. His elbows were angled out, and he was running his hands back and forth on the ground. His fingers were splayed like a fan rake, and he picked up and scattered the soil as he ran them along the ground: hands left and up, head down and right... I took a step closer, and heard his sweet quiet, ...singing? I listened, relished that dear voice, and was ready to say 'David...', when I heard her come up beside me. I looked over. She held up a finger, crossways to her mouth: wait...

We stood together as he ran his fingers up and flowing, through the rows, scattered the dirt, bobbed his head...

...if not me, then who...?

... *and we turned to each other. I asked with my eyes, hoped with my soul. She nodded. Once, for both: to show she knew, and also to answer. With a nod.*
'Yes, of course. I'll be sure...'

Gail

A quiet room, two matching chairs. Evening.
It's been snowing for hours, and we sit, in our 'apartment'. When we started to work on this place, I realized that he'd already built it. In his mind. Joined, by a breezeway, to the back of 'the house'. It went up quickly, and was soon just another part of the Ostrander place. Unremarked, and carelessly christened; no time was wasted here on reconsidered names. The house, the garden yard, the old barn, the new orchard. When we framed up the walls, he named a purpose for each room as it came into shape: eating, sleeping, sitting…
The chairs are dark green, and face west; to a wall with the wood stove centered between the tv and the big window.
Sit, look, say to myself… the words I see:

Wind whips white, while we watch. Whistles and whirls, …out in the dark. Whispers. How many words for what wind does? Whines, wails, waltzes, …*time there was* when I knew? Hardy? Simon? …some poet. Swirls, screeches, strains, cries… / …wind cries *something*, and the phone rings. …was a time, I do remember. Rings: we look at each other and wait. Rings again, and Adam plants his palms, one on each chair-arm, ready to rise. 'I'll get it.'
Beats, blasts, and blows of course… nothing friendly comes to mind, and he's back. 'Steph', and I look up and wait. 'She says forget trying to get in for tomorrow. They've pulled the plows already, and the buses…' Lashes, scours, and I miss the rest. I've heard all I have to, and a pause means my turn. 'Luke and Jakey's idea of a perfect winter. No school—unless they walk there, …as if. Friends over for shimmey. Steph feeds. Gaming after lunch. Life is good.'
He opens the stove barehand, puts a log on, pokers it into place, and sits back down. Us, …silence, …sitting safe in the dreamy eye of a huge

winter storm. Four days after we plowed out the last one. Silence,—except for the tapping, whipping, blowing, crackling... and we look at each other. 'Although no hockey if I don't get in and plow.' I think, for a second, and no, there's nowhere to take that. I pick up my book.

He stands, stretches; waits, and paces. I look up, and he's watching firelight shapes on the walls as he walks. In the low light... dancing, jumping, flicking... and *Mary* it is, *Cries Mary*, comes to me late, and he calls from the bedroom. 'Want a sweater?'

'I'm ok...' and I glove open the stove-top and put another log in. He comes back ... sees the fire going strong, takes his sweater off, re-checks the walls, sits down, and looks at the rumpled sweater in his lap. I'm well entertained by this theatre. He picks up the remote; aims at the tv. 'Let's check the weather.'

That's a good one. Earns a chuckle. 'That's a good one. Look out the window, listen to our house creak,... time to be your own weatherman, isn't it?'

He laughs, lightly. 'I know that window too well', but he looks at me instead of going ahead and clicking the tv on.

'...or maybe another channel?'

'You know exactly what you'll see on the weather channel. And we may not get *any* channels, in this.' He points the remote at me and mimes button work. 'Ok, what's on the Gail channel? I need distraction.'

I make a weather-girl smile, and angle my hand, palm facing the weather-map window. 'It's snowing again, for all of you out there who are locked in windowless rooms. Double the usual this winter, and none the one before. The weather just keeps getting weirder. As of next summer, we'll officially have more words for drought than Eskimos do for snow. The government is considering putting icebergs on the endangered species watchlist. Back with more of the same after the break.' Lower my forearm to turn the palm up and open, to the man in the other chair. 'Over to you, Adam.'

He smiles, sits, looks... and I go back to reading.

But the big lunk is a dead-right lunk, damn him; again. Winter is dragging, and '*Feburary one is just the half done*'. They say. He picks up the clicker again, and spins it slowly between his thumb and index finger. 'I'm not tired. And I'm too tired to read. Alternatives?'

We sit still, and listen. It whistles, higher, ...whips snow on the windows and off the walls, whirls, wails, ...and it comes to me: sudden but sure, from wherever this kind of thing keeps itself hidden.

'March fifteenth will be fifteen years.'

Jumped out, made a face and said 'boo'—the years number, that is. The time with him. This place. His family. It all rattles around in the wind and the old house and my mind on long snow days passed inside—days like this: drifting into night, shapeless and slow.

'Is it really, ...I mean...will it?' His firelit face is a perfect expression, unwilled, of computation.

'Um hum. Our so-called anniversary. Shall we celebrate? We could pass the time planning a party.' Bad joke, or maybe none at all, since technically I'm probably still Mrs Bob Ruggerio, ...unless it counts as 'until' when you're parted so long it's like death did its job. All of which leaves us where we started: looking out at winter and ahead to days of nothing to do but talk weather with Alma and David at quiet dinners and then again after, with each other, while we sit.

'Fifteen years. Do you remember anything from that OFA lecture?' I ask; he thinks.

'It was March 15.' I look 'try harder', and he does. 'Grey folding chairs ...and the heating system was so loud it drowned out Dr. whatever his name was from Guelph.' Thinks. 'The back of your head, of your hair, of ... whatever. How you were ...so blond...'

I smile, and take my turn. 'You had to leave early the next day ...didn't want to leave your parents alone too long with your brother. You said ...nice meeting you...'

He waits; I'm the one who keeps our stories straight. 'You do know that I coloured my hair then?' His face says *no way*.

We both laugh, and he speaks. 'Fifteen years...a long time. Although sometimes it seems short, too.'

Yes, I think; yes, it's both; and say '...yes, lots has happened...', ...and then, from the same hiding place as *boo*: '...what do you think the next fifteen will be like?'

Pops out with a made-up white halloween face. Gotcha. Jolted my thoughts to quick shaky wondering. What else is waiting there?

He waits.

This could pass some time. 'Well?'

His thinking and waiting gets us nowhere. It's up to me.

'Imagine us then. Fifteen years from now. So much might happen. What will it be like? Then.'

Adam should never play poker. His expression is a pure picture of a practical man trying to picture something that can't be loosened with a left ratchet turn, ...and frustrated by his complete inability. I laugh out loud, but not too loud. The wind whips, the stories I tell myself flicker on the walls, ...and I volunteer.

'Shall I tell you?'

He shrugs 'whatever', knowing full well that I can't, and aims the clicker. He can't imagine that I can imagine. It spooks this steady man, a solid guy with an unimaginative imagination. Smacks of tea-leaves and ghost stories, and so I have to ask.

'Wouldn't you like to know?'

White flakes on the dark window; bright yellow fire in the dark stove; storytellers clocking in for the night shift. I remember how it's done. I was one. Bob called us 'we', the *brotherhood*, which should have tipped me off.

'Wouldn't you like...' is the lure. The line is played out and we wait for that feeling: the soft tug of a bite, to that trolling question: '...to know what happens?'

We reel it in, just a touch...and sometimes, on a lucky evening, the hook gets set.

Adam nibbles. 'Probably not.' The answer itself doesn't matter; a '*maybe*' is good enough. '...likely some reason we're not supposed to, even if you did know.'

Wind drops to quiet, and I jig. 'Maybe not, and maybe I don't. But imagine I do.'

He puts the clicker down and we're still, matching club chairs angled to the fireplace and the table between. Look together past worn green carpet, up the wall with the dimmed lamp plugged in, and on out to night.

'Ok, so tell.' Resistant. He's not there yet, but almost.

Rises to gusty again, sharp, and I can't, yet, but almost. Tell. 'That's not how it works. I can't just tell. It's a certain kind of game. You have to ask.'

Bitter, whistles high, and he thinks. Slow, as he must. Catches on;... blusters, whirls. He takes a breath and starts with an easy one.

'Fifteen from now?'

I nod.

'We're here?'

I imagine. 'You and me? Um-hm.' I work on it while he thinks.

'Apples?'

I think weather. '...yes and no...'

We wait together while the room shrinks to a small two-voice-holding firelit ball. He works carefully: folds the sweater he's been holding and bends to stow it under the table: looking away to ask the one that says yes: imagine it for us. His voice flickers. 'Alma?'

The game is afoot.

I shake my head to the side of his head, and look at the answer: 'Ten years now.' Blows softer now, whispers, dies down for a minute. He didn't look, just felt my head shake. Did he know?; he doesn't ask more. I lead the story along gently.

'...and Emily the year after...we're both orphans now.'

Back again with a roar, rattles the window. 'Roger too, that same year.' Feel him looking in the dark. We turn our eyes—to the window. Flakes tap, pile up, are twirled off, and we look back at each other. He sits, face set, with no expression I can read in profile.

Howls now, in snow twisting gusts, and I look at what I'd seen and said so far, and all I'd committed myself to say. Roger, Emily, and Alma, ... Alma, and deep Adam asks 'Was it easy?'

It never is. I shake my head without looking at him. I could ask 'for who?', but the questions are his, is how it works.

'Is this true?' I shake my head, slowly, think 'maybe', but don't answer. A no answer meaning wrong question. Meaning try again. Howls higher, cries its own cry, and he asks '...must have been hard on David?'

'Very.'

He's silent; it piles rage on its rages; and I add quietly: 'But something good came from it.'

He looks up. I catch the movement in the side of my eye, and look over and see that he misunderstood. 'From how it affected him, I mean.'

'Which was?'

I look away to imagine. 'He was upset, of course, and sort of ... reverted. Alma told him in a matter of fact way, but he didn't want to hear it. You talked to him, said he had to try as hard as he could, but he cried and waved his arms and couldn't stop jittering. Nothing helped, and that only made things even worse for Alma. And for you. Then Amanda and her boyfriend had to move down east for his job and she and Miranda had been fighting and Dorrie had another stroke and it was everything at once and we had an idea.'

I looked away and knew he was looking at me and didn't know if he knew 'we' meant 'me'. Probably he did. 'David and Miranda moved into Dorrie's. They took care of her, as best they could, till she went into care. Miranda got him to join the choir at St Andrew's, and even took him to church when it was empty on weekdays. And his piano lessons were easier from town. He joined a big band at PECI. It really was the right thing. Settled him down and he had something else to think about. They're great friends. He and Miranda. He's still David: watches reruns, sniffles if we talk about her, but otherwise ok: sings, practices on his keyboard,...cleans the house and the yard. I think he's happy.'

That was the short answer. He worked on it. Slowly, as he does with everything, in the just-us storm night story space. Silent, in the vast groaning howl. Still, as it died down, got ready and he asked, slowly as he does. '...and us?'

I'm a sharp listener. The 'and' was barely there, the 'us' was emphatic. Final; and I asked. 'What about us?'

It was part of an answer, since there was an 'us' to ask about. He knew the right question. 'We're here?'

I looked at him and then away. 'We're here.' I looked at him and then away; he didn't ask. He'd done his part. I let it wash in: the years, with his odd family and not odd enough neighbours, moving from city to orchard, from a one room apartment to spending time outside, from writing about big ideas to every other sentence being about wind or rain. The hundred vague Glebe memories to the hundred clear little blurbs I tell myself everyday in this everyday house. All that, and all the other bits of air I had ready to retool into words. All in rows and columns, with a line below. I added them up. Closed my eyes and looked. The sum was us, ...and a picture.

'Adam', I said, and said what I saw...'Us...here, ...with the wind. In this room. Sitting, and...

...late November light hit the window and the wind fell to quiet. You stood up. 'Shall we take a look?' I nodded, stood too, and we went out.

Stepped onto the porch, stood side by side. The warm, easy breeze swept dust and gulls along in the three o'clock light, and we stood. Pink sun through the weed maples and down the drive some project on the go across the street; and we looked. Turned together to face past the driveshed and up the slope; and we looked. Stepped down the steps and walked, side by side, up the lane.

Shorts and t-shirts; no need for socks. Another board blown off the driveshed. You picked it up, turned it to nails-out side down, and stacked it on the others. 'Tomorrow ...screw these back on...' Walked, side by side, and we looked, up the slope. Knowing what was up there was no better than the last time we looked, and the year before that, and how sad we are seeing it all and walking up anyway. Angled shadows on the dry grass and the old flatbed behind the driveshed. Battered plywood boxes stacked up and sitting empty in a row.

We got there and no, it was no different than last week. A few of the trees still held withered leaves, and most of their little apples. Pink and tan and pocked and wormy...and sad like us. We looked down and over to Smith's and up the slope and everywhere but the orchard until there wasn't anyplace else to check out; stood and stared. You grunted and walked up a row, raised your arm and swept it along as you moved. Stopped, picked an apple, looked for a good spot, and bit. Spit. 'Ugh.'

I tried sympathy. 'They're not that bad?' You tossed it up the row and spat. 'Sorry, worm.' You looked at the rows. 'What do you think? How much in all? Not that we'll waste our time picking.' I thought, guessed. 'Half a box.' I scanned the rows. 'And nothing to do with them , even if we did.'

I looked back at where you'd been, and saw you heading up the east row- the one with your latest experiments. I walked to where I could follow your back as you looked down at the young trees, and then ahead to what you were looking at: three small trees at the top of the row actually had a not-bad little crop,—not nearly as many pocks and black spots as the old ones.

You went over to the deadfall, picked off three limbs, came back and wedged one into the crotch of each of the healthy trees. I watched you bend, gingerly, as you picked one of the good ones, and went on up the row. You stooped and checked another 'apple bush', and turned around to look back down the lane to the house and the street. The sun was dropping behind the pond, chill now, …and a whiff of smoke …sharp, and pleasant. It drifted away and I tried to name it, …it was…/heard you behind me… turned around. 'A few of the Jonah-22-Spy crosses actually did ok.'

I had to squint into the last sun to answer. 'I saw.'

Your face and the treeline were dark against the orange-pink horizon. 'I think maybe we can graft straight Jonas back onto that stock.'

I nodded. The wind and the smell and the chill. 'Let's go back.'

We walked, and you talked. 'The three new, and a few of the old, if we're generous for sentimental value. And a few branches had ok fruit, sort of.' We crossed into the shadow of the drivshed, and it got cooler still. I wrapped my arms around myself. 'We're basically starting all over again.'

I nodded. Three years without any real crop sealed the deal.

'Maybe we can find some other trees to graft.'

I nodded again, and looked on down the driveway. Fish, that was it. They had a smoker going, and the smoke ran along in a low cloud, across the street and up the driveway. The minimill was turning, too, and the blades spun little blurry clouds of reflected sunset across the west field. We stood and watched and smelled.

You: 'Maybe Rona wants a crack at the apples?'

That made sense to me. 'Sure. I'll mention it. Maybe she'll help you graft.' You shook your head. 'I can do that. There's no weight involved, and… if it's not too damp a day.'

I didn't say anything, and you carried on. 'It's bad enough without your making it worse.'

I said something. 'No lifting, please. And I'm cold.' We went up the steps. You reached out to open the door and it opened toward us, ahead of your hand.

'Hey guys.'

'Rona.'

She held up a wrapped package. 'Just got a roast. Jason's friends are here. Big dinner.'

I went past and got my jacket off the hook. You looked at the package. 'Big and frozen. Cooking that on wood?'

She nodded. 'But I'll saw it up first.'

You laughed. 'Good plan, or it's dinner for Christmas, ... maybe.'

I was more practical. 'Or just nuke it here? Five minutes and you're good to go.'

You laughed again, and teased her gently. 'Maybe Jay could hook up a circuit for a microwave off the mill.' She batted it away. 'Just what we need—another jerry-rigged circuit for another derelict appliance.' Pause. 'And another job for Jay.'

You smiled and went on into our apartment, and Rona and I went into the old kitchen. I put the roast in the microwave, set it to five, and we sat at the table. She looked tired, but asked politely. 'How have you been?'

I listened to the microwave going in the dusty house, thought about how we'd been, and went for the easy answer. 'Fine. You?'

'Good, busy. Lots of fish. Maple's decided to learn to read. Etcetera. Life...'

I'm sure I had that kind of drive once, but couldn't remember what it felt like. 'Do you guys want to glean the apples? There's not much we can use.'

She was lovely, in a soft, young, plain, brown hair brown sweater way. 'Absolutely.' Genuinely happy. '...that would be great. They'd love it.' They meant Berta and Maple. Always. The timer pinged. We got up, she opened the door, and stopped. Stopped and stood for a second in the way of somebody making a plan. Took two old blue striped tea towels out from the upper right drawer. Took the drippy roast out, set it on one and wiped the pan of the microwave with the other. Folded the second around the first. Knew what was where in the room where the fridge motor hummed alone. Knew that I wanted her to help herself. Never knew Alma and blue stripes and why we'd left the kitchen as it was then. I knew they'd come back clean even though we didn't need them. We went out, and walked down the driveway together.

I stopped before she went across the road. 'Enjoy your dinner.'

'Thanks.'

She took a first step; stopped, and thought about it before she spoke.

'Jason's friends are looking for a squat.' Pause. 'The ones who are visiting us now. A longer pause, and she spoke tentatively. 'If you and Adam have any ideas.'

I was surprised, and then thought maybe I shouldn't be. 'I'll mention it. Are there a lot...?' I hesitated, and realized that after five years of being friendly neighbours I didn't even know if they called themselves squatters. Like we did.

'Absolutely. Klaus says that things are getting way worse in the city. Worse than they're saying. Although he always talks like that. The sky is falling. He says next summer he expects hundreds. A mass migration. Hopefully not, but he says that's why they're here now—beat the rush.' We were both shivering now as it got dark, but she seemed to want to talk about it. 'Come on over and meet them. She's a chef. Was.' She held up the roast. 'She can't wait to cook this on wood.'

I thought, and decided. 'Not now. Maybe I'll come by tomorrow? Or bring the kids here and we'll pick. Supposed to be warm again.'

'Sounds good. And thanks. Even though you said not to say.'

'Bye.'

We didn't know what to do with ourselves that night, and there was lots of it to fill. You researched the Jonah 3A- Dry/Spy cross, and read postings from your group about ways of keeping an orchard 'fruitful' through drought, pestilance, and blizzard. I read an article on marketing jellies and preserves. Eight o'clock. Read it again, and decided: no, not for me. Eight-oh-eight. Put down the magazine. 'Anything good on the net?'

'Maybe. Look at this.' You showed me a blog from a couple who had developed a nice crab-apple graft which was doing fine in soil that stayed dry for months at a time. They made great jelly, ok juice, and were delicious canned or served with chicken. They were selling cuttings, and offered a sample dozen to anybody who would come and get them. You started writing to them, saying what you'd tried with the crosses. 'This is what we need...and here's one from a nutter up in Bancroft. Trying to graft mini-Cortlands onto *riparia* root stock. Says it should be able to go way down for water...'

I didn't want to watch. 'I'll do the laundry. We've almost got a load. Give me your socks.' You gave, and went back to typing. I got the basket, and went through the breezeway and into the house. I was thinking of the kids across the street and maybe working with her this weekend and I turned the light on by the washer and no, David's choir was this weekend and I got the wash in and going. All this tangled, cluttered thinking meant there was something else I was supposed to think, and the pump kicked in and jolted the empty old house. I hooked the drain hose to the grey water cistern. Alma never wanted to spend on a new washing machine. We should make an effort to take Jake and Lukey to the concert. Rona and Berta did their wash by hand, outdoors. Those A22 crosses would take five years to bear fruit, at least. The tub steamed in winter, and they poured it out to make a rink. If they were all they were cracked up to be, the crosses, and if the grafts took. The pump stopped, and the house was quiet. I went back out, into our living room, and sat down. You typed for a minute, read something and saw I was sitting there doing nothing, ...realized that doing nothing was my way of waiting, and stopped and looked. I thought I'd just say it, but it didn't come out. I tried out a few lead-ins, to myself, and felt how wrong they were. You stood up, went into the bedroom and came back with two sweaters. I took mine, and said 'We should think of some other way to use this place.' We put on the sweaters and I carried on. 'Those grafts will be years away from fruit, and the work is hard for us now.' You closed the programs and we looked at the screen saver. A deer in the orchard last winter. It's head was angled—just ready to bite a frozen apple. 'What else could we do?'

You had a point, so I did all I could do, and ignored it. 'Let's at least try to think of things.'

You looked at the deer and spoke to me. 'Ok'; kept looking.

Not at me speaking practically: 'I mean we should at least talk about it.'

At me, finally, at least, although still with your stubborn face: 'You talk; I'll try to listen. I don't have anything in particular to contribute.'

At me backing down: 'Another time, then. But think about it.'

Past me, then, at nothing: 'Anytime you're ready. With an idea.'

I got up and went out to get the laundry. I hung out it on the new white metal and old wooden racks in the old kitchen and went back in. You were back on line. 'Look at this—a pack frame manual sprayer—free.'

I looked at the ad. 'If you want to drive up to Tweed for it.'

You scrolled down.

Our books were on the table. The old green club chairs faced the tv in the corner, below and to the left of the window; they always had done. The fluorescent was on in the bedroom and the doorway glowed. Another quiet room, and I spoke quietly in this one. 'But think about it.'

Ten past nine. I sat and tried to think of the something else.

Days later it was December, still warm, and I was still thinking.

Thursday is shopping day: a trip to town. I look forward to it, although somebody hearing our checklist of things wrong with town would never think. Gas costs a fortune...like we said it should. Food is expensive... although we always said it was too cheap. We were proud of being able to improvise with what we had, and said people have too much junk, but there's always some part or fitting we need. And the people...town seemed to catch and hold everybody who couldn't really come to grips with where things were going—the too old, too tired, too poor. Or too pig-headed, I thought but didn't say—that kind of negative comment didn't play well around town. Another unspoken rule with a deep taproot: you had to stalk your prey for at least a generation to earn the privilege of taking a shot at it.

Expensive and depressing, but we liked lumping it. The FSPO tanker delivered untaxed 'farmer's gas' on Wednesday, nine to noon, in the lot where the store used to be. You got your farm card, in case the driver was new, and took two plastic fiver's down for a fifty cash fill up. Half the town price and last us a month.

I walked my Wednesday rounds.

Cloudy, rain in the air?, and cool enough for a fleece. The first stop was Mary's, three houses up—she's the last of your old neighbours. No cars. Sumac turning red. Silence. I opened its big door as I walked, and let myself in. A red fox ran out of the brush and across the road. I'd raised the subject—the next move was yours. Weeds were taking over her driveway. I could see her grey bob bent over the loom as I turned the corner to the house. I went up to the window and waved until she looked up. She wasn't startled, just held the shuttle and pointed around to the door. I let myself in, took off my gumboots, and went on through to her studio. She smiled 'good morning' and kept on working. I went around the loom to where she could see me.

'Got your list?'

She nodded toward the window-sill, 'of course'—and I picked it up and looked. Sugar, tea, flour, and baking powder. Her old lady scrawl on the pad with the pencil tied on, with a length of red yarn. Sugar, tea, flour... made me think of a shopping list from Catherine Parr Trail. I tore off the sheet with the unnecessary list, and wrote on the next page: 'No cat food? Buck off his feed?'

She read, and nothing in her face said it was anything special. 'Just getting old. I think he's bored.'

I wrote. 'sure? It keeps ok', and held it out for her.

She nodded. 'We're fine for now.'

An odd vibe. Did she think I meant that she was losing her grip, and resented the intrusion? The house smelled like old people, and was dusted here but not there. I felt uneasy. She'd said they were fine for now. I said it to myself, felt uneasy, looked around the room, but nothing gelled. I wrote 'see you tomorrow', and put the pad down beside her.

She read, wove, smiled, and nodded. 'Adam has always been helpful; since he was little. And you too, for as long as I can remember. Literally.'

I closed the side door with the body English it takes, and thought I'd try to remember to ask you to have a look at it, the overgrown driveway, and heard you say that she never goes out anyway.

I walked back up her curved drive, felt a ping in the air, and swung my arms to brush the pine boughs. The lower ones were bare, and at arm height they'd grown in to just about within arms-spread-apart of each other. Never cut back. I thought of Adam complaining about getting the truck down, and read his part for him. ' ...cut them next week. No, we always liked helping them. I helped him plant them and now I'll cut them back. The driveway should be passable. When she has to call an ambulance she'll thank the guy who helped it through. If she wants to curse me out between now and then, it will be an amusement. We can invite the kids over to watch. I'll even give her the limbs for firewood.'

That conversational monologue got me to the road. I turned left, back, walking into the sun. The leaves were brown and dry, a few on trees and some underfoot. Smith's dog barked, alone in the house again. Breathe deep: rain, soon? Up the slope was the orchard. The new rows of test plantings made straight lines beside the texture of the grown in trees. A shotgun pop from the river side, below the hill, and clear in the damp air. A gust, and then smoke from Rona's wash kettle hugging low over their garden, just before I turned the bend and saw her and Berta wringing out a sheet. They were half turned away, ...singing something, but I couldn't catch it. Korin's bike was leaning against one of the garden frames. Wes and Les supervised the washing from rain barrel perches: black and marmalade, sitting backs arched in mirror symmetry, ...a tail flicked. Bronze and gold in winter sun.

I spoke loud enough—...'morning, ladies...'—to get them out of their song/dream, and they waved as I walked up the drive. 'I'm here for your list. What's that song?' Berta took the sheet over to the line and turned sideways to answer while she walked. 'It doesn't have a name. It's just the way White Cloud talks.' Talking white clouds?

Rona put more stuff in the kettle and pushed it around with her washstick. 'It doesn't sound so bad when you sing it. Go on in. Meet our friends. Claus and Debbi and Hope and White Cloud...'

She looked at Berta. '...and one on the way. They're working on a name.' She looked again, which she likes doing. 'What's today's, sweetie? Hopscotch, or something?'

Berta was hunched into her hoodie. She had a nice little spark. I liked her. Good timing, too. She waited a beat, and updated her mother's stale news. 'That's overly yesterday. Today they're decided to let it name and re-name itself...' She changed her voice to floaty. '...to celebrate each awakening.' Laughed. 'And Korin's here too.' She imitated Korin's off-key trill.

Rona made a vaguely disapproving face and Berta went back to laundry work with a sharp snap ahead of each nicely hung article and I could see how Rona felt her soul fly with each *crack!* in the damp air. Her face glowed with pride and joy when she spoke. 'I've got the list and money ready inside. Go on in. On the desk. We'll be in as soon as we get this stuff hung up.'

'OK,' I thought as I turned. 'Will it be dry before it rains?'

Rona sniffed. 'No, nothing till tomorrow late.'

Berta wasn't so sure. 'Cutting it close, mom.'

'Too late to turn back now, sweetie.'

Pride and joy, all over her face, and I turned sideways to hide the look on mine. Got it arranged as best I could, and went onto the deck and in through the patio doors. Roger had hung up an old blue velvet curtain just inside the doors, hoping to block the living room from nosy eyes and outside cold. Rona and Jay had left it there, and now I pushed it out of my way. Went in, to today's variation on the usual bedlam. 'Old Roger's place' looks small from outside, but has room for a world of chaos. Crazier than ever today. A young woman in a puffy black quilted jacket and striped scarf squatted in front of the cookstove, working a bellows. Old Otis lay next to her, dreaming dog dreams? Expectant Debbi? Must be. Mr Debbi was pouring water from a bucket into a kettle and shouting at kids running around hitting pans together. Piles of packs and blankets.. and an Underwood! Korin was tuning a guitar-like instrument. (Remember her? The little blond girl from behind the fire hall? Her dad drove into the millpond after the late shift? From the hill at Scott's dam?) Definitely homemade, and I thought: or was it only tuning? She waved and smiled over the racket. 'Hey Gail.'

I waved back and already started thinking of good excuses to leave. Or any. One of the kids fell, and there was a still moment where we all watched it lying there, and waited for the tears and wails to start. My heart broke. The place was cold and messy and smelled like smoked fish and baby shit; it kept on beating while it shattered: completely, to pieces. Mr Debbi went over to the wailing kid, and put his face close to ..hers?, made a soothing sound, and, she clamped her little fat fingers in his blond hair. The crying stopped, and he turned back to me. Weak smile. 'Hi. I'm Claus.'

'Gail. Pleased to meet you.' Nods only—no way to shake hands.

A new bout of crying, louder than before, and Claus turned back to the baby. He reached down, 'Cloud', and she stopped again. I went over to the desk in the corner and poked around for the list,—but no dice. Rona came in from behind the curtain and waved. 'Sorry...got it right here.' In her pocket. 'Here.' I took the list and she reached back in her pocket. 'Here's fifty. That should cover it ...and our share of gas and hydro.' I looked at the list and thought how much like Mary's it was. Except for wool. *'Trade for wool.* What's that?'

'Oh yeah. For thirty-aught shells. Tom needs, and Jay's got lots. And we need...' More crying interrupted and it was starting to warm up in the room. Debbi had the fire going. I turned back to Rona. 'You don't owe us anything for gas and hydro. We go in every week, and we'd keep the freezer running anyway.' But I did think *'good manners'.*

She was turned sideways, getting a little bag of shotgun shells. I put a five back on the desk, and moved a rock to hold it down. 'I wish you'd keep it. You may need it.'

She laughed. 'Spend it now, neighbour. It's worth a little less every day.'

I thought that might be a new variation on some bit of homespun wisdom, but she lowered her voice and carried on. 'Debbi says a new batch of inflation is on the way. Her brother is in Ottawa. Not supposed to tell, but...' Then lowered to a whisper. 'Part of why they're moving out here.'

I didn't need to hear any more financial conspiracy theories, but was interested in the potential new neighbours. 'How do you know them?'

'We don't really. Not that well. They're friends of Jay's, from school.'

Berta came in through the curtain and went over to the cookstove and rubbed her hands together. Korin strummed and sang, and the kids moved over to the couch and sat in a huggy little lump. Claws scratched my stomach. Rona smiled. 'Let's have tea.' I sucked tears back into my eyes and stood up straight. 'Thanks... but no. Got to help Adam. Another time.'

Maple slapped the window and shouted. 'Deddy come deddy.' All the kids went over. Jason came in and everybody cracked up.

He had an orange hunting cap on sideways, and twigs and grass in his beard and sweater, and a broken shotgun by the barrel. Rona shook her head. 'My higher primate.' Jason did a Tarzan thump—dirty hands on his old sweater chest—and deepened his voice. 'Show some respect for the man who tames nature. See me stand upright. The great white hunter is victorious!' Everybody stopped and looked. 'Yes, victorious. The animal kingdom bows in awe and supplication. Next week we eat meat.' Rona had to hide her pride and joy again. 'So where is the victim, oh great hunter?' He did a Neil Young voice. 'Down by the river. I shot my supper.' Then back to normal. 'Only I need a hand getting it home.'

He looked over at Claus. 'Male bonding time.'

Claus was skeptical. 'This is like, a fully-grown wild animal? We're supposed to drag a carcass up the hill and over the fields? It is definitely dead?'

'As a *doe-nail*.' Born ham. 'And I've got the cart ready. Come on, we should bleed this guy, ...I mean girl.'

I started to go out with them, but Rona and Debbi went out into the entryway with me and Rona put a hand on my sleeve when I was on the other side of the curtain. 'So we'll see you tomorrow with the stuff from town?'

I nodded and put my fleece on. Rona looked down, ready to speak. I waited. 'Did you have a chance to think about...' They both looked. '...or to ask Adam if there's any place... house that's been, ...or might be... free... he knows about where we could stay for a... squat.'

I didn't want to say that I'd forgotten to mention it.

Debbi spoke up, like somebody who had one important thing to say and finally had a chance and the courage to say it. 'We really need to get out here. And out of town. We have some bills and...'

I nodded, and really did feel sympathy. I arranged my fleece for going out, but she wasn't done. 'We have a lot to figure out, you know? I mean about how to live. So we'll need to ask sometimes. I mean we'd help too.' She had no idea. '…but if somebody who didn't like squats called us in…' I reached for the door-slider handle. ' …and Claus was in the facebook group from one of the Monsanto hackers. He left before the bombing, but…'

Now she had my attention.

' …running down every list…taking hard drives, doing audits, looking for charges, children's aid…it's getting… bad. Even if he doesn't have any job right now that he could get fired from for it…'Kids shouted on the other side of the curtain. There was a catch in her voice. 'I mean not fired for anything real, just because the mounties or cops were asking…it's… I'm rambling…he's …we're …scared.'

I'd sized her up wrong: she needed a big cry, not a talk. I listened to her half choke at the end of the stuttery sort-of sentence, and remembered other almost-but-not-quite crying scenes. How many words were in those not-speaking faces and reaching hands. How Emily's face went blank when I told her about leaving Joe, and the miscarriage. 'Darling…' Blank and pale, meaning 'let's not…', how I knew in that second: *don't,*—and held on to the tears. How silent Alma had put a hand on each of sitting David's forearms when he twitched: be strong, try hard. How Rona was looking behind Debbi, over to me. Wondering why it took so long to come up with an answer?

'I'll ask him.'

And I did; ask you, that is, but not right away. We'd talked about the squatters, but not that much. We knew a few, slightly, and knew about some others. You called it a *'local matter'*, and passed along the gossip when word went around that another vacant old place had smoke in the chimney or sheep in the yard. If I asked for details, or what you thought of it, I got nothing. '…place was deserted anyway. Falling in on itself.' Or a shrug. '…Not causing trouble for anybody but themselves.' We didn't seek them out. They were younger, and had a community of their own. Not our business.

When I got back, your boots were in the mudroom, but no jacket on the hook. Why?

Inside, you were sitting at the table, check shirt, slumped… - obviously dead beat. The furnace was on for the first time this fall. Looking down, hands in your lap under the tabletop. I stood behind you, ran my hands down your back, and bent my head onto yours. 'Grafts?' A nod, and a sound that meant yes. I reached around and took off your jacket. To hang up. To not talk.

You showered, we had dinner, and you put the heating pad on your hands, and still looked tired. I sat down opposite and reached for my book. We sat for a few minutes, and your face relaxed as the heat did its thing for your fingers.

'How many did you do?' You closed your eyes to answer. 'Ten. I think that's all we can get. And got the seeds from that fruit...it's in the freezer.' That was a first. 'Who grows apples from seed?' Rhetorically, but you answered literally. 'Nobody I know. Or ever heard of.'

You took your hands off the heating pad to make a hands apart, palms up gesture of ...? Acknowledgement? Apology? Admission of foolishness and plea for indulgence. I thought that of course we'd never pick one apple from any of that, took a breath to form the words, and ...but why point out what you already knew? 'They're in ours or Rona's?' The heat kept working, and you flexed your fingers. 'Ours. Labeled.' Those gnarly fat fingers weren't designed to sort seeds.

'I can help, if you want to save seeds.'

You nodded. 'I know.' Sitting, tired, where you sit every night. 'I needed to think.' Nodded, looked up at me, having provided an explanation for spending time on a pointless task. I looked at your red fingers flexing: a slow, cumbersome approximation of the way that motion works on smooth young hands. 'And the grafts all under glass.' You'd felt the northeast wind too. It came to me a minute late—that damp was why your hands were so bad. You squirmed in your chair, looked away, kept talking. 'Maybe your were right.'

Years of experience taught me to think back to what conversation had been left hanging recently, and not to ask '...about what?'

You saw me trying, and helped. 'About us, here. Apples.' Picked up our talk from last week as if those passed few days were a normal pause in conversation. 'It's hard now, and I can't see it getting better. I just don't know what else we can do. To make a go of it here.'

Did I feel relief or apprehension? I felt lots of something. When I first raised the subject it was conversational, a gambit. 'What if...?' Coming from you it was solid and wrought: an offering. I examined it. You waited. That pause was part of the conversation. No different from the pause between where we left off last week and 'Maybe you were right' a minute ago. We could reach a consensus tonight or next year. But now that you'd said it, there was a danger of it happening. My stomach felt light.

And I did want to help, but I'd been over it with myself and ruled out everything I'd come up with. No need for a mechanic out here, with so many cars driven away, for good. No jobs for shop teachers, even if it wasn't too expensive to drive into and back from town every day. A nursery was a possibility, and we could do the grafts and potting up and so forth, but starting up a retail operation...? Now, with us older, the customers gone...

I came out of this daydream and saw you waiting. Had you been waiting for the past week? 'Could we try hiring help? Keep it going while we work on new crosses? The kids coming in might want the work?'

I thought of all kinds of flaws in this as I argued it. You saw them, too, plus ones of your own. 'Find the right ones. Teach them what to do. Get them here and back. Home, I mean. Keep on experimenting and hope that the experiments work well enough to pay them. And soon enough. And that the weather doesn't keep getting even crazier—to the point where no experiments or results will be of any use. And even if we got it going, suppose some bull goose loony gets in as mayor and decides that the government should get its groove back by hiring his brother-in-law's security firm to clear out them all out?' You saw me not following exactly. '...our wetback squat labour force. That leaves us *all fruit and no pickers*.'

That was quite good. All the ideas in order. I had no idea you'd been taking such a hard look at it. I must have been getting slack. You were alone with grafts and seeds all day. I looked over at you looking down, then looking up. 'Ok.' I digested a little more and knew that if you'd worked it out that far, you'd probably taken it even further along. The best way to hear the rest was to talk gently around it till it hatched. We sat. I thought. 'We don't have to rely on just fruit. We own decent land, outright. We could grow a bigger garden. Our house is solid; we can live cheap.'

You nodded yes, let's think; and yes, that's this part of the discussion; I'll say more when it's time. I thought no, I must not rush you; no, we're not giving up apples, yes, we thought side by side in the quiet getting dark and rising wind and I remembered, yes, now was a good time.

'Jason and Rona have friends staying there, too. Claus and Debbi and two kids. Younger than theirs. I met them today when I went for the list. Oh, and he wants us to stop at Bill and Cathy's tomorrow—trade shells for wool.'

You sighed. 'That's quite a crowd for Roger's.'

'Indeed.' Take it slow. 'Bedlam.' Easy does...'They seem nice. Actually, they want to move down here. She's pregnant. They asked if we knew of anyplace ...vacant.'

'Sounds dumb. Why would anybody want to move into some dilapidated old shack...pregnant, winter coming...like maybe tomorrow...to do what?'

I hadn't thought it through till I heard you not do the same. 'I don't think it's a matter of wanting to. I mean I just realized that now. I get the feeling they have to.' And I remembered the northeast bite up Mary's drive and the southwest smoke of the washerwomen's fire. *Christmas is coming,* David said...*the geese*....

You nodded, and I thought yes, *have to*...'It's not like Jay and Rona. There's something deliberate about their plan. Even if it's idealistic. These other kids look desperate.'

You're a better listener than talker. But that helped me. What made them seem so desperate? There wasn't much here, other than deserted farms. Although they were free. Get away from ...maybe it really was worse out there than we'd thought, ...?

'...the shells already?' I wasn't being a good listener. '...get going first thing?'

The weather answered for me: bang. Bang; the sound we hadn't heard in months pinged on the roof. We stopped thinking and listened. Twice now, then four, four hundred and we smiled and welcome-backed the rain that had been away since early May.

'This should be a good one.' It was a formula; either of us might have said it.

It came hard and stormy. We sat and listened as it pounded the roof, bristled the trees, hailstoned the windows...

Listened and thought about what we should do, as weak branches were blown off limbs and into the night. Lit the fire and sat. Sat and went to bed. Went to bed and tried to sleep as we thought about what we should do. I waking-dreamt 'turkeys?' and probably smiled in my half-sleep. 'Maybe mumbled to you. Remember how the Bongards hated birds?' I turned over, pulled up the cover. Complained about them. Dreamed about Alma telling. Smelly, sickly, noisy...foxes...and went back to sleep. Woke yet again and heard the sump pump from the old basement. Sleet sounds and half-woke-up. Looked at the windows frosting up in the dark and pictured the fields sucking water till they were full and the water still coming and I must have finally gone solidly back to sleep because it was grey light when I heard...'shit'.

I looked over to see what time it was.

It was no time: the clock light was out and you were standing. ...flick the switch.. no light...'shit' again; ...dreamy warm ...pulled the duvet up...thinking something; heard: '...no hydro.' You were getting dressed, and I heard the breakers being flipped in the kitchen and '...nothing'.

It was just light enough to look out and see it still raining, dotting a field of standing water—from the house all the way over to Burrit's lane and beyond. I was cold and sleepy and I heard you going out ... and then I was awake. Why the furnace hadn't come on?

You called from the door. '... foot of water down there and no hydro to run the pump.' The door closed and by the time I got dressed and out to the breezeway you were back from the driveshed. Soaked, and with the little 12 volt pump and a coil of drain line. 'See if you can get the spare battery.'

I got gumboots and raingear on while you worked on clamping the line onto the pump. One of the doors was blown off the shed, and it looked like the mimimill had lost a blade too, -it was still spinning off balance. Me too, walking in the muddy dawn rain.

I sloshed back with the battery, and you weren't in the breezeway, so I went on through the kitchen and the laundry and saw a light in the basement.

'Is the hydro back?' I started down the stairs: sideways, to allow for the weight of the battery, and heard you say 'flashlight' as I stood on the bottom step and saw the water over the top of your boots. 'Oh my god.' And tried to get serious; fast. It was more than a foot. You were holding the light between your knees and trying to work on clamping the sump hose to the electric pump outtake valve.

There were more jobs than hands. I hoisted the battery up onto the lip of the old cistern, and waded over to help. Water, in my boots. You didn't say anything. I picked the flashlight out from between your knees and took the pump out from under your arm and put it under mine. Freezing. Everything was. I angled the light to shine on where you were working. Cold water ran down my boots and up my socks. You tightened the hose clamp and let the joint fall in the water and put the driver in you back pocket.

'... the battery?' I pointed the light back to the cistern ledge. You took an adjustable wrench out of the same back pocket as you walked over to the cistern and played out the hose. My hands were numb. You took the pump out from under my arm and rested it on the ledge next to the battery, and used your handkerchief to clean off the terminals. 'I can't see plus and minus here. See if you can get the light in close...' I stood close and angled it over. 'ok...good.' Your hands were red. 'Ok, there.' You placed each line on its right terminal and slipped the wrench over the nut. 'Ok—right on there.' You pinched the wrench adjustment thread, and it looked like you were trying to lift a truck with two frozen fingers as you tried to close the jaws to the size of the nut that would bind the cables onto the battery. Cold, dark, and 'fuck...!' as the wrench slipped off. Splashed into the freezing water, and your numb fingers caught nothing when you reached in for it. I aimed the light, passed it to you, pushed up my sleeve as far as it could go, reached down, ... and got it. You nodded, and steadied the battery with your free elbow while I cranked the nuts on tight. The pump whirred quietly as it started up. It was a long run through the two lengths of hose, and it snake-shook as the water started to pass through and finally reach the sump line. I let myself feel relief and how absolutely freezing and soaked I was. You looked so miserable I had to look away.

We went up; left our dirty boots and soaking socks in the kitchen, and went into the old house and on through to the living room. We stood in the far corner, where you can look out the window and see the tail end of sump line running out from the basement. The sheet of steel roofing it spits onto had been blown away, but water was shooting out the pipe and running on away into the lake that was our front yard. We watched: seeing it work was all I needed. Time now to go back for dry socks and a fire going; and still you watched. I went back out through the dining room and looked at the big old piano and peeked into the den. Dust everywhere and mouse shit on the lazy boy and I didn't hear you behind me.

'Adam?'

Nothing; ... why not? Louder. 'Adam.'

You shouted back. 'What?' From where?

'Where are you? Let's get back.'

No answer. My bare feet freezing on the cold floor. I went out and around through the living room to the bottom of the stairs, heard the sound of me in the empty, and looked up at you standing in the hall, ... shining the flashlight into Alma's old room.

'Are you nuts, man?'

Your head was in her doorway, and when you turned around and looked at me I thought you might have been hypnotized. 'What?'

I'd been ready to keep up our shouting conversation, but that look stopped me; and I spoke quietly instead as I shivered. 'What are you doing?'

You looked at the flashlight, and switched it off. 'Probably don't need this anymore. It's daytime now.' A trance voice, not talking to me. You came down the stairs, wiggled the newel post, and I looked at your twisty red hands and mussed up hair and big red feet with black toenails and soaking cuffs and dreamy eyes. 'Flies everywhere up there. Windows are black with them.'

I reached out, and took the light. You hadn't turned it off. 'Let's go get dried out.' You came back to life, almost.

'Chilly in here, eh? Takes days to get these old places properly warmed up and an hour with no heat to cool them off.'

We went back 'home', lit a fire, and I put the kettle on the woodstove. 'Should boil soon. Tea?'

'Yes, please. Definitely. I'll take a gallon, please.' You were wondering about something. 'What's up?'

'That's a lot of water, and it will keep coming for who knows how long and who also knows how long it will take to get it back on this time?' I saw where he was going. 'The hydro, you mean?'

'Um-hm. We can use the truck battery next, but after that we'd have to run the truck to re-charge.'

We looked at the kettle, and I put another log on. 'Maybe Jay could recharge off the mill?'

You rubbed your hands together over the stove. '...what I'm hoping.'

We drank tea and sat. Dried out, warmed up, and half dozed.

Everything felt disconnected and remote, as if we didn't know what day or time it was, and the phone rang. That snapped us out of dreamland, and you were talking.

'...right. I guess so. I completely forgot...no, nothing like that, just a flood and no hydro...I know...back on? Good. Yeah, I'll get by this morning. She can shop while I come by. Ok.' I followed the part about it being Thursday and were we coming in, and you filled in the rest. 'Steph says a poplar came down in Dorrie's yard last night. Into the garage door. David and Miranda called her.

'Do you have the lists?'

Of course I did; you knew that. 'Why didn't they just call you? Us.'

You knew. 'They might have...They might have just called the number in the speed dial. With no hydro, we've got no machine to take the calls.'

Right. 'So they want you to deal with it?'

'Um-hm. Should be ok. Or you look like no?'

I felt like no. No going shopping, town, or anyplace else. But bed.

You stood up and looked outside. 'It's let up. We can go.'

I thought of reasons why not. 'What about the truck battery? Do we need that for the basement? And the roads?' I was just talking. If you were determined to go, that was that.

'Let me see where we stand.' You went out and came back with an update.

'...still no hydro, but the tractor battery lasted long enough to pump out most of the water, so we're ok for a few hours. We can drop off the tractor battery at Jason's on our way out.' I was limp and still felt damp, but trying to stop you would have been like trying to stop a glacier. The power came back for a minute, lights went on, and the clock flashed 12:00 for a minute, and then it all went off again.

Sometime, a soon after but still un-numbered time, we had the chain-saw and all its gear behind the seat, gas/oil mix in the bed, and the pump battery on a rag in my lap. You backed out the muddy driveway, turned around, drove ahead a few feet and pulled into the kids' front yard. A light double-honk: Jason's face popped up in the window, and he waved 'come on in'. I was all wrapped up in parka and gumboots. 'I'll sit.'

You took the battery, went in, and came back in a minute with a different wrapped battery, opened the door on my side and put it down gently on the cloth. I was still half asleep. You put the truck in gear and went out their yard and back up our drive. 'What's up?' You pointed to the minimill lurching around irregularly in the breeze. 'Blade got blown off last night.' Of course it had, I remembered. 'Jay lent me theirs. Says he'll charge ours up when he gets the blade back on. ' You parked the truck by the door and took the battery. 'Back in a flash.'

I clapped my hands and rolled my neck. No way of getting any sleep today, best to wake up and get to it. Errands to run. Errands... I need money. Ok, awake, get organized. I stepped out of the cab as you came out of the mudroom and looked 'what's up?' 'Forgot the money.'

You half smiled. 'And I forgot to check.'

We finally got our show on the road. The main road, today. No back road shortcuts in this weather. The fields were flooded everywhere: light brown water rippled in the breeze and gushed over the falls when we turned onto the main road and were aimed at town. A maple was down just past where Grimmons used to live, but somebody had already been by and gleaned what would have been blocking the road. The main road was higher and clear. It felt safe now, and I could start to plan.

'So...will you cut the tree while I shop?'

You shook your head. 'I'd like to wait with that, I think. Jay wants me to stop in at Crappy T and price a new blade. The one that blew off got bent up. Man, they were all huddled around the cookstove there playing some board game. It's got to be hard. He needs a bag of sand mix and light bar oil. Maybe I'll do that while you shop and we can go to Dorrie's after. Is that ok?'

I thought about Rona cooking for all them, and Berta being an assistant mother instead of hanging out with kids her age. 'Sure. Fine. I'll talk to David and Miranda, catch up. And the wool...don't forget.'

Town was quiet; somehow even more lonely and deserted than usual. Somebody had looted more of the Coronet: that didn't even rate a comment. It rained again, and stopped again. We were the only car at the light, and sat while it went through its five-corner cycle. You pointed up ahead: Two flashing OPP cruisers and a lane blocked. When we got there, they waved us by. The roof had blown off the old bakery, and it sat tipped sideways and ripped open; half in the KFC lot and half on the road. You tooted the horn 'hi' to one of the cops roping off the site with yellow tape. West of town we did our errands, and went back above Main and along King. Branches down everywhere, and a few people out trying to unblock sewer grates. More lonely and deserted than usual.

We came down Paul, and you pulled up short of Dorrie's. It was a spectacular fall, timber!, an OMG image. The poplar had been rooted on Hansen's property next door, but blew down sideways across Dorrie's driveway and front yard. The upper part blocked the walk and a limb and its branches were wedged up against her front door. The root pad stood upright, and had taken out most of Hansen's driveway when the wind peeled it off. Higher than the truck. We sat there and took it in. It seemed funny when we tooted the horn and got a face in the window for the second time that day. David waved, and pointed to the fallen tree.

I waved back, and you got out of the cab, opened the jump door and took out the chainsaw and held it up so he could see. He clapped. You fired it up without checking anything, and nipped off the branches which were bent up on the door. I got out and headed up the walk.

You couldn't have run the saw for more than a few seconds to get that limbing done, but that was plenty for town. Hanson and the new neighbour on the other side both looked out their doors: curious...something happening? I went on inside and looked back out the sidelight. They were both pulling on jackets and hats as they limp-walked over to the action; ready to chat. You topped up the gas and bar oil while you talked and they pointed at the standing root. Miranda and David came in from the den and we watched the show. As soon as you had the saw all set up, you put your headphones on and got down to business. The neighbours talked and gestured while you started bucking things up. We got tired of watching after a minute and Miranda offered to heat up soup, which sounded great. You were back in twenty minutes. '...all done. That smells good.'

Miranda started to go for a bowl and spoon, turned around and said 'thanks' as she walked, and came back with your lunch. 'We take you guys for granted.' She put your bowl down on Dorrie's big oak table, and the sound of it landing echoed. Ordinary sounds are big and musical in the minutes after a chainsaw has stopped. You reached for the spoon, picked it up, but couldn't really grip it firmly. It fell, clanged off the table and again when it landed on the floor. It was nothing, a dropped soup spoon, but it clanged and echoed and we watched. Miranda went to get another one and I looked at your face as you reached down to pick it up. Unexpressive, stolid, which meant you were suffering. Miranda came back, and I tried to think about something else. You gripped the spoon carefully, and ate soup like a man who'd missed breakfast. David sang soft scales, up and down and up. His 'practicing' voice. Like a bird, I thought. I was too tired to be like anything.

'Delicious.' You put the spoon down, tilted the bowl up, drank, and were done. You looked at Miranda as she cleared the bowl and spoon. 'Hits the spot. And you should.'

Not knowing your conversational logic, she wondered. 'Should what?'

'Take us for granted.'

Miranda looked surprised, so you explained. 'We're your family. We should leave you trapped in the house by a maurading poplar?' David trilled his scales and she laughed and asked. 'Do you want the wood?'

You shook your head and made a maybe yes maybe no motion with your left hand. 'I think we're good. Our place doesn't use that much. And it's just quick heat. Garbage wood, really. Rots before it dries.'

David stopped singing, and looked up. 'Doorbell.' He whistled a bird call.

You and I looked over at him. 'What's with that?'

He made the call again as he went to get the door. 'A lovebird.'

I turned around and looked at Miranda, but she was looking away— picking up the soup bowl. You were thinking out loud. 'Maybe the kids want it for their washtub fires. Or smoking. Actually, that's what it's good for. All their fish.'

I hardly heard you: I was watching Miranda turning away to the kitchen with the dishes, and the back of her neck was a lovely bright pink. Well well, ... a lovebird?

David came back, still tweet-whistling the birdcall into a tune, and followed by a tall boy with curly blond hair and a guitar case. They stood in the archway. We all looked at each other, and nobody knew exactly where to start. A boy indeed. He was quite a nice looking young man. Very blue eyes. Just needed a shave and a haircut, and ...you were looking at him like you knew the face.

Miranda came back in the other door. '...hey, X.' Nice smile, and I thought that even you could see what was happening here. 'This is my aunt and uncle. Adam and Gail.' He blew her a kiss across the room and nodded at us. 'Pleased to meet you.'

David went out, and the sound of the piano came in from the den. You reached out you hand, and he put the guitar case in his left hand to shake your right. I read a carefully painted-on motto on the other side of the case: *From the ruins of 4/4 time are built the tunes of eternity!* Not a bad one...how did it really go? *From the ruins of...* no, I didn't have it.

There was other writing around the edges. It would come to me when it was ready. You smiled, looked, and asked. 'Is your last name McGuire?'

He smiled back, 'Francis Xavier MacGuire -McKee...is, was, and always will be...' and you kept smiling too as you asked. '...related to Terry?'

'Sure. Uncle T. Haven't seen him in years.'

You shook your head. 'I used to work for him. Shelagh's your mom?'

His answer was quiet. 'Was. She died last year. Peking Three. I've got the house. We do, now. With my brother.'

'Sorry. I didn't hear. Where's Terry now?'

'No idea. Went out west, did the tar sands. Didn't even make it back for the creamation. Kind of a worry, actually, since the flood. Fort Mac got hit hard, too. But I just don't know.'

We sat, and listened to scales on the piano. For a minute, maybe, and you looked restless. 'We should get going. Groceries and hardware to deliver.' I stood up. 'And wood.' I went to the hall to get my coat and turned around fast to get a look at Miranda. It was just a quick one, but there it was, all over her. Waited till she 28 before she found him, and he turned out to be a sweet scruffy guitarist with a letter for a name. I turned back to the coat hook, and was so tired that didn't even feel it coming. That tear. I wiped my eye, one quick one with a pinky, and put on my jacket: ready to go.

I said goodbye to everybody while you backed the truck up to the bucked up tree and lowered the gate. I was out the door and starting down the walkway when I saw your face as you lifted the first heavy, wet round into the bed. 'Adam.'

You straightened up slowly; looked over when I spoke. 'Don't be mulish.'

You looked over and saw that I meant it. 'I'll get them to help.'

Nobody talked while we worked. Two of us lifted each round onto the open gate, and you arranged them running front to back in the bed. You closed the gate, and we drove out of town: down Bridge Street and up the hill. It would be dark in an hour, and the clouds had blown on out to the southwest. The sun would set under them, any minute now. We drove past the Cressy turnoff, and the burnt out house where the dentist used to live with the chimney left standing. Drove by slowly, and looked. You had gossip from Dan, '... working at Crappy Tire now. Says they say he shot himself after he lit it. Wife left him just before, not been seen since.'

That was the end of the story.

Goats from next door walked through the...ruins? One stood in a window frame. Just stood there, billy-goat profile in the ...and it came to me: *from the ruins of time are built the ... castles of eternity...* and it all came to me. All. Landed in the truck, a puff of unshaped air, sat there in the middle, knew where it was, and grew. I thought it over as it made itself comfortable, filled the space between us completely and exactly: grew around us. Over my left, and your right, arm; made a perfect shape up our sides. I looked, studied, and: yes, that was it. The road bent, and turned us to angled into the sun. You lowered the visor, and I looked at your red-grey stubble face and the lines in your cheeks in the raking light. 'Adam.'

The lines in your cheeks, you looking dead ahead, squinting as you drove and waited and listened. I said it direct. 'Let's give it to them.'

The man I love doesn't grumble 'What? Give what?' Mumble '... talking about? ... to who?'

I slid over in the seat; right over: I could feel you concentrating: there was no space between us.

We passed the Black River cutoff and angled onto the road home: right into the sunset. Still water lying in the fields reflected orange and pink and dark, through the road maples and on to the treeline in silhouette. Exquisite beauty. You were working on it, *grinding slowly but exceedingly fine*. I was completely exhausted. Spectacular colours. We passed Miller's. A magnificent sunset. A lovely evening. How Emily told her guests it was time to go. *Thank you so much. This has been a lovely evening.* Passed Dowdell's... his even though he's gone, ... almost home.

You shifted down and turned to back into the spot at the side of Roger's where they stacked their wood. Jay and Claus saw or heard, and came out. You rolled down the window. 'Load of wood for you. Junk, but its free.'

They guy laughed. 'Get what you pay for.' 'At best.'

You opened the door and stepped out, and looked at the last of sunset. 'Let's do it now, before we can't see where to stack it. '

I opened the door and got out; looked at them. 'Can you guys do it?' I waited a second. 'Adam's back isn't great....'

They'd started by the time I tailed off. I wondered to you if we could take Mary's stuff over tomorrow. 'I'm bushed.'

You nodded, nodded; and they were done unloading, that fast. You remembered. 'New blade will run you two and a quarter, Jay. Come over and try to hammer out the old one if you want. Sand mix on the back seat.'

We drove home, finally, home. The hydro was back. It was cold, but the fridge hummed, the lights blazed, and all the clocks flashed twelve. You put the chainsaw gear away and I unloaded the shopping. I put Rona and Mary's stuff aside, turned up the furnace, and sagged into my chair. Flashing clock, dvd player, stove, and I dreamed... *it was a cold house in December, and all the clocks flashed... thirteen... ?* and I dozed.

We lit the fire, made dinner, didn't say a word. My words sat there, waiting. The house was warm and lit and back to normal, except for my

words. We had a glass of wine. Alma rolled over in her grave as you sipped. I waited for you. Finally: '...talk about it tomorrow?'
Yes.
We can, tomorrow. I only needed to know that you knew.

Tomorrow came, and I had second thoughts. You reset the flashing twelve's, and we had coffee in the chairs we'd almost fallen asleep in the night before.
You started without a preamble. 'Have you been thinking about this?' That didn't quite make sense. '...for a while?' And then it did, more than before. I explained. 'I must have been. Without really knowing. But it didn't come to me till yesterday. Clearly.'
'And it's clear to you now? Give it away?' Flat; a direct question.
'Not so much. Or not the same. I'm feeling stronger for having slept.' But I was sure, to a point. 'We have to do something.'
You nodded, and shook your head. Which left me to keep it going.
'Maybe we could sort of... share it... work with them somehow... ?'
You kept nodding and shaking, slowly.
'...or scale it all back somehow... ?'
And even slower, 'We've been over it, and back over the back over.'
While I ran down the last appeals. '...all our work... it's such good dirt...'
And stopped. Your face went to solid as I talked. '...might miss it, later, in a way... ?'
Solid, and I knew what was coming. 'If we have to do it, let's do it.' Was how you did things. 'Now, ...or soon.'
I wasn't ready for that much decisiveness. I should have been. That's you. '...we'll just spend the time stewing about it. Let's put it into figuring out what we'll do.' Years were slipping away, and now I wanted to hold on. Arguments popped up, reasons for one more try. 'Are we sure they'll take it'?' But slipping is what things do. 'Will they even be able to figure out what to do?' Away.
You laughed. I remembered other laughs. 'They'll make the same mistakes we did. Unless we tell them how not to. We can show them how to graft, and leave the hydro account set up. Whatever...'
Once I let it in, it made itself at home. 'Can you actually give somebody a farm?'
'I guess so. It's ours. I don't know how it works. Maybe we still hold the title to the place. Or lease it to them for nothing? If they pay the taxes, great, but who's going to foreclose a place nobody will buy... for back taxes nobody will pay?'

They slipped, fell, and flowed. I felt lightheaded as I pictured years and apples and Alma and I sat, watched and they stopped. It wasn't a flood, they just moved a little way away and bobbed there: comfortably at home. You sat, and I saw your eyes blink. '...they'll work it out. There are lots of them and they're young. And Jay is bright enough.' Yes indeed, and sharp-eyed Berta too; and I thought of those clever little hands learning to graft and plant and I smiled.

'So we'll tell them tomorrow? I mean ask?'

'Or today. Before we get cold feet. Like yesterday.'

We're only planning the rest of our lives; and I get Ostrander humour. If that's what it is.

'Today, right. Of course. I have to take their stuff over.'

'Um-hm. And Mary's ...and their battery.'

'Maybe both go.' How we talk. '...and then all we have to is decide. What we'll do...next. Go to live.'

We sat, and the idea of giving away a home kept making itself at home. We'd built this apartment, ourselves, *out the back*. Onto what then became *the old house*. Years with Alma getting quiet, David playing piano, singing, and...and I knew. 'I can tell you.'

You looked up. '...tell me...?'

'...where we can go.'

You waited.

'Dorrie's.' I could have just said it all at once, but I felt like moving slowly, and this was how your family did it anyway... so I let you object.

'No room for us there. Town makes sense, but there's only two bedrooms, and it's a small house.'

I shook my head. 'We'd be doing everybody a favour if we moved in.'

You really hadn't noticed! 'Everybody...? What favour?'

'She's staying there because she thinks it's the right thing to do. Miranda. Take care of David, keep the house.' It was so simple that it was hard to explain. Put things in order for somebody who had to grasp them that way. 'X is the one. She'd love to move in with him. She doesn't want to upset David by leaving or moving him...and doesn't want her family to lose the house.'

I looked at your face to see if I needed to keep going. No, I couldn't tell, so I stopped. It would come. We sat.

Friday December fifteenth: the weather that morning was back to normal. The new normal: warm and dry again. Everything was set up and ready to go. Everything we could think of. We were half packed, and would leave it that way for this stage. David didn't have any concerts until Christmas Eve, and the idea was that we'd go in today, have dinner with everybody, and explain the change to David. Miranda and X would go to his place after: stage one of a slow move.

We'd decided to leave the houses mostly as they were, and had explained most of how things worked 'to the kids'. Pumps, cistern, the washing machine they wouldn't use, 'probably'. Furnace, woodstove, breaker panels. Today was to be orchard, gardens, and go. Us. I stood on the porch and watched them walking up the drive. Them. Rona had asked if they could all come today, together. 'We can show the place to the kids. They don't completely understand.' The kids' kids.

Up the long driveway they came. A scraggy line. Jay and Rona led, walking and talking. Debbi, pregnant in silhouette, carried Hope on her shoulders, and Maple rode a little bike. White Cloud seemed to be shouting at Claus as she walked just behind him. Her arms flailed—some crisis. Berta was last, head down, fingers of one hand tapping at something small and electronic, and the other throwing a stick to Otis. He brought it back and she threw it again.

We were ready. Light jackets, sneakers. Ready to meet them at the top of the driveway, before they came inside. Our house. Dusty morning, brown grass; we all said hello. Where to start today? We talked weather. I realized I'd have to get it going.

'Why don't I show you the garden?' See who took me up on it.

I half turned that way and took a first step. Rona followed; Debbi noticed, and shifted Hope. You nodded to Jason and looked over to the driveshed. '...show you guys in there?' And things got moving.

I imagined the driveshed talk—it was all there in a flash. Where things were and why that arrangement was right, and how to change anything about it was to risk disaster. Fluid levels. Nut sizes. Blade connections.

I did the garden, with the sense that I was running on. Why potatoes should go in the back garden and lettuce in the side and where the old window sash attached to the side to make a cold frame. I caught a little smile from Rona and a look sideways at Berta from Debbi, and stopped; almost mid sentence. 'You know this stuff, already...' Polite smiles. Rona: 'Sort of, but still...missing one thing might be all it takes to lose a crop.' Blessed are the kids, for they shall inherit the earth.

We saved the orchard for last, and all together. We thought it would be the hardest, but it turned out to be a cheerful procession walking up the laneway in the sunny morning. The kids' bright jackets, ochre leaves on a few trees, brown winter dirt, and you pointed out '...that pink chunk of granite, by the fir, is a gravestone. Sam. My brother's horse.' I was drifting;

letting it go; under *blue skies, nothing but,* and you explained how things stood, in tree-by-tree detail.
'...the new ones, the A23 cross. Prune them way back. A third of the crown a year, at least.'
'...these are the ones from 2 years ago—they fruit late, but that might be ok for now. Good deep roots. Tolerate almost no water...' Jason looked, listened, said nothing.
'...these three of the old ones still have some...' Berta and Claus walked up the rows of the older trees, found an apple and tossed it for Otis to chase. Why was he out? '...maybe keep for sentimental reasons...?' Maple cried and the mothers wandered off, back to...the house that they'd just go in as if it was theirs...and I looked around: at this strange place which was becoming a little more not mine with each look, newer and stranger with each...Smith's field that was, the back of our house that needed painting, down the driveway to Roger's and the minimill, around to the millpond and back to the orchard where you were making a chopping sideways motion with your hand and Jay was nodding and asking something. Letting it go, years of pink and gold and blue and *my brother's keeper*...and I turned around and walked back down the lane. Rona was on the porch with Hope, and Maple rode in circles. 'Debbi took Cloud in to the bathroom. She thinks it's a marvelous novelty. Cloud does.'
I opened the mudroom door and held it for her. Them. 'Come on; I'll show you around the kitchen and be hostess, ...mum for tea.' Maple cried and I looked away. Put the kettle on.

Rona seemed awkward sitting while I worked. 'Sit', I said.
Maple came in and I rinsed tea things. Tea, milk, sugar...I'd brought in from our house. Cups and spoons and what all had been in their places in this room since before I'd first seen it. Some of them looked like they could have been there before Alma first had seen it. I held up a tarnished teaspoon to Rona. 'You might want to cull this collection.'
She didn't say anything; just looked at the spoon, checked Maple, put a hand on Hope's shoulder to stop her from running in the house.
I wanted words in the air, and asked Maple: 'Are you all ready to move?'
She looked down at her lap, and mom answered for her. 'Absolutely. We all are. We start lugging tomorrow. We'll take the front; the back will be easier for them, with the newer stuff...'
Their 'front' is our old, their easier is our 'back'. '...all settled in by Christmas.' She was still hesitant, and I wondered why she didn't say anything. Maple ran on into the house. Rona sat quietly while the kettle finally boiled. Finally said: 'Gail, this is so amazing. I know—you said to

stop saying it, but I have to. It's unbelievable. A godsend.' What a lovely old phrase. She sighed. 'There. That's it. Last time.'

I thought: that's ok, I was listening to other sounds. Kids running in the dining room, banging on the piano.

I got the kettle off and warmed the pot and we had tea in the living room. Or tried. Serving tea to mothers looking after children is folly, and I was the fool. The kids jumped on the stuffed chairs, and raised old dust and they sneezed. I couldn't remember the last time we sat in those chairs, put cups on those tables. I showed Rona plugs behind the sofa, said the windows didn't open, …she watched the kids run and barely listened. When I stopped it was quiet, for a second and she looked around the room. 'I've got an idea.'

We waited.

'Let's do a big Christmas dinner here. Bring David and anybody else from your family you want. Big venison roast. And Korin…we talked to her about a beach party dinner, but this will be way better.' Maple kissed Cloud and said 'I hate you.' She ran out and then back in.

I heard myself talking like Emily. 'What a lovely idea.' And thought that it really would be. 'We've more or less given up on all that stuff. I'm not sure we'll remember the drill.'

Debbi looked ready to nap. She and Hope sprawled in an armchair. White cloud climbed onto her lap and stage-whispered to mommy. 'I love the new house.' Mommy stroked her hair, and looked down. The little choking sound. Rona sipped tea. Held the cup upright, carefully, thumb and two fingers, in a way I remembered. I never knew where she was from; other than 'the city'. Looked at me and spoke in a tone I knew well too well to ever forget, from *ages ago*, truly from a former life. 'I'm so happy I could purr.'

And that did it. Debbi held Maple, whispered 'honey' and let it go. An ocean of tears. Weeks worth, all the flood that she hadn't been able to cry while she tried to hold it together, across the street. Months of cold, broke, worried, pregnant. All that and who knows what more?

Rona and I looked at each other, nervously, …offer a Kleenex?, and they rained. Poured down her face till it gleamed. We looked, unsure at first…and then us, too. Maple and Hope and Cloud looked, and joined in. Wailing, keening. I was embarrassed and wanted to stop and couldn't. I tried to laugh, coughed, and then it really was embarrassing. You and Jason and Claus and Berta were packed in the doorway. Four packed bodies and you and Jason talking at the same time. Your deep '…what in the name…' and his stage voice over. 'Sweet biscuits, it's a coven.'

He looked up, invoking the heavens? 'Leave them alone for an hour and they're calling the beast and all his followers and attendants up into the house.' He stepped in, raised his arms, and intoned. 'Begone...'

Berta turned and went out, the kids went to their dads, and we got it back under control. For a minute, till the laughing started. Berta came back in and gave Rona a look. She calmed down. 'OK, honey, we're going.'

They sort-of regrouped and it was the kind of leaving where you don't say good-by. I watched them walk and ride and be carried down the drive. How many women had mothers who said 'purr' and 'lovely'?

Afternoon. We had the truck loaded and wondered if we had everything we needed and if we'd left things here in order, and it didn't matter. We were going fifteen minutes away and weren't due for two hours. We'd be back at some point soon. They'd call or email if they had to ask about something. Or would they keep the phone? I should remember to ask.

We changed our clothes twice and kept finding one thing to check before we left. All without discussion, and then we couldn't find anything else. We looked around and at each other, and seemed to know what was next. We walked up the lane and stood at the bottom of the slope. Looked at the orchard from just outside it. Turned around and started back down, and I remembered. 'I forgot to tell you. Rona has invited us all for Christmas dinner. David and Miranda too, and anybody else we want to ask. Maybe invite Steph and the boys?'

You stopped walking and looked back at the house. 'Maybe.'

We walked on to the truck, and each opened a door. We stopped there and talked across the hood. I wanted better than maybe. 'I don't know how she'll get it all organized with the kids and just moving in and all, but isn't that sweet? Venison. A real big extended family Christmas diner, all the kids, some of their friends...'

You looked at the truck and the house and the ground. 'I don't know.' Stood there with one hand on the open door, looking over the hood at me looking surprised.

'It might upset David to see other people here. Strangers. And it's so chaotic and noisy and smelly with all those kids.' Moving past the door to get in and not even looking at me. 'It's hard enough to think about coming back here at all, much less...'

I don't know what *much less*. I don't know what all else the problems with coming back and Christmas were. I couldn't bear hearing. I didn't want to see you saying them, no matter how good any of them were, as reasons. I saw my grey hair and pinched face in the truck window and let my thoughts boil.

Does he have any idea? After all these years, the slightest clue? The loudest, smelliest, most disorganized chaos, venison, drinking, crying, applesauce, fighting, ...could he really have that much no idea at all?

After thirty years? And then I didn't want to know and looked over to see if he knew and...he was sleeping. Jaw slack, head back, hands in his lap. The snow had stopped and the room was dark and perfectly silent except for a tiny snore. Sleeping. Like a baby. How long had I been talking to myself while he slept?

...but I wasn't talking. When did the story slip over, into a dream? I didn't remember and I remembered the fifteen or thirty year ago afternoon when he came to pick me up at the train. We'd written and talked and met once more in six months since the conference; and then a call. Would I like to visit? See the orchard, meet his family?

October. He was waiting when I got off. The old CN stations look alike, brick with overhanging roofs. He leaned forward to take my suitcase and we stood on the platform, facing each other. Seconds passed. Had I had a good trip? That was such a lame start to a big date that I laughed. Tip-toe stood, arm to his arm, and kissed his cheek. 'I'm happy to see you, Adam.' He laughed too, and we walked to his truck.

We drove out of town, over a high bridge, and into the County. I told it to myself the way I would have written it. Drove south under wind shaped clouds driven east over east bending fields. Jersey herds and a black barn. Burning leaves, and their sharp smelling, cone-shaped smoke. Through a soft, golden-tipped marsh: a sea-field. It flexed and parted to make us a path. Flowed back behind and melted together when we'd passed. Two hydro trucks blocked a lane, and I gave my small news: how my mother was doing in the home, how I was fed up with COG infighting. We watched landscapes in the windshield in comfortable, optional silence, like a drive-in. We went through a town, turned off the highway, and drove to a smaller town. It was lovely, and I said that. I started to say that I'd decided to give up on being a writer and—, and he cut me off with a deep breath—it felt like he'd planned to speak at exactly that point. His dad, ...he'd had a stroke, and didn't get around very well now. Got gruff sometimes. I nodded. We crossed a bridge over a small dam and he said his mom was trying to carry the load and bundled it all up and worried a lot and was easily upset and didn't sing much anymore. We pulled into the tree-lined driveway of a large brick house. Heavy looking, in the way those houses can be. Orange and purple in October sun and shadow, with an old-fashioned porch on the side, and he said his brother was a bit 'different'. Brittle, sort of. Bright, in his own way, but fragile. Joy and pain and things went right to him, or through him, or something. So this was what he'd been waiting to tell me. Unsure. Serious. Working up to the words he'd worked out for the occasion. 'He's eight years younger.' He stopped the car at the side of the house. I thought all that called for some answer. Nothing came to me as he cut the engine, and sat looking at me. I wanted to lighten it up. 'And you? What do you have to tell me about you?' A throwaway,—it sounded wrong as soon as its air became words, and I tried to fix it with a smile as he looked. A laugh, and I gripped the door handle with my right hand as he looked. Looked, and reached. He took my small left hand, definitely, with his right. Held it, and my heart jumped. The house had black shutters and white trim, and the side door opened. A lanky, sandy, smiling boy-man stepped onto the porch and waved both arms over his head. The wind shivered the poplars along the drive, and he pressed my hand, like he meant it. I looked up the hill at the neat orchard rows of shadows bigger than the little trees that cast them. The wind gripped my heart, twirled it, and I wondered: hold on? The solid brick house, us in the car, the boy-man's thin raised arms, your rough hand, my heart in the wind...let go? Stood, sat, waved, pressed, ...spun up the shadow patterned afternoon rows and was gone.

CPSIA information can be obtained at www.ICGtesting.com
Printed in the USA
LVOW11s0104090616

491647LV00001B/20/P